"How do you know my father?" Fiona's voice sounded as raw as it felt.

"I don't. I never met him until this day, although I grew up hearing tales about him and my father. And I know who you are, Fiona O'Rourke."

A terrible roaring filled her ears, louder than the blizzard's wail, louder than any sound she had ever known. The force of it trembled through her, and she felt as if a lasso were tightening around her neck. Her dreams cracked apart like breaking ice. "Y-you know me?"

"Aye." Gently came that single word.

"But how? Unless you are—" Her tongue froze, her mind rolled around uselessly because she knew exactly who he was. For she had grown up hearing those same tales of her da and another man, the man whose son now towered before her. "No, it can't be."

"Ian McPherson. Your betrothed."

Jillian Hart grew up on her family's homestead, where she helped raise cattle, rode horses and scribbled stories in her spare time. After earning her English degree from Whitman College, she worked in travel and advertising before selling her first novel. When Jillian isn't working on her next story, she can be found puttering in her rose garden, curled up with a good book or spending quiet evenings at home with her family.

JILLIAN HART

Gingham Bride

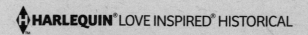

HARLEQUIN® LOVE INSPIRED® HISTORICAL

Recycling programs
for this product may
not exist in your area.

™ LOVE INSPIRED BOOKS

ISBN-13: 978-0-373-78945-0

Gingham Bride

www.Harlequin.com

Printed in U.S.A.

I trust in the mercy of God forever and ever.
—*Psalms* 52:8

Chapter One

Angel County, Montana Territory,
December 1883

"Ma, when is Da coming back from town?"
Fiona O'Rourke threw open the kitchen door,
shivering beneath the lean-to's roof. *Please,*
she prayed, *let him be gone a long time.*

A pot clanged as if in answer. "Soon. And
just why are you askin'?"

"Uh, I was just wondering, Ma." *Soon.*
That was not the answer she had been hoping for. Her stomach tightened with nerves as
she set down the milk pail and backed out the
door. She wanted to hear that Da had gone to
his favorite saloon in town for the afternoon,
which would give her plenty of time to fix the
problem before her father returned.

"You are still in your barn boots?" Ma

turned from the stove in a swirl of faded calico. "Tell me why you are not ready to help with the kitchen work? What is taking you so long outside today?"

The word *lazy* was not there, but the intonation of it was strong in her mother's fading brogue. Fiona winced, although she was used to it. Life was not pleasant in the O'Rourke household. Love was absent. She did not know if happiness and love actually existed in the world. But she did know that if her father discovered the horse was missing, she would pay dearly for it. She had school to think of—five full months before she would graduate. If she was punished, then she might not be able to go to school for a few days. The thought of not seeing her friends, the friends who understood her, hurt fiercely and more than any punishment could.

"I will work harder, Ma. I'll be back soon." She scrambled through the shelter of the lean-to. Wood splinters and bark shavings crackled beneath her boots.

"It will not be soon enough, girl! I've already started the meal, can't you see? You are worthless. I don't know if any man will have the likes of you, and your da and I will be stuck supporting you forever." A pot lid slammed down with a ringing iron clang. Unforgiving and strict, Ma turned from the stove, weary in her worn-thin dress and apron. She raised the spatula, clutching it in one hand. "When your da comes home, he will expect the barn work to be done or else."

It was the "or else" that put fear into her and she dashed full speed past the strap hanging on a nail on the lean-to wall and into the icy blast of the north wind. Outside, tiny, airy snowflakes danced like music. She did not take the time to watch their beauty or breathe in their wintry, pure scent as she plunged down the steps into the deep snow. She hitched her skirts to her knees and kept going. The cold air burned her throat and lungs as she climbed over the broken board of the fence and into the fallow fields. Snow draped like a pristine silk blanket over the rise and fall of the prairie, and she scanned the still, unbroken whiteness for a big bay horse.

Nothing. How far could he have gone? He had not been loose for long, yet he was not within sight. Where could he be? He might have headed in any direction. Thinking of that strap on the wall, Fiona whirled, searching in the snow for telltale tracks. The *toot, too-oot* of the Northern Pacific echoed behind her, a lone, plaintive noise in the vast prairie stillness, as if to remind her of her plans. One day she would be a passenger on those polished cars. One day, when she had saved enough and was finished with school, she would calmly buy a ticket, climb aboard and ride away, leaving this great unhappy life behind.

In the meantime, she had a horse to find, and quick. But how? It was a big job for one girl. She lifted her skirts, heading for the highest crest in the sloping field. If only her brother were still alive, he would know exactly what to do. He would have put his arm around her shoulder, calming her with kind, reassuring words. Johnny would have told her to finish her chores, that he would take care of everything, no need to worry. He would be the one spotting the hoof-prints and following them. He would know how to capture a runaway. She lumbered through the deepening drifts, watching as the snow began to fall harder, filling the gelding's tracks.

How could she do this alone? She missed her brother. Grief wrapped around her as cold as the north winds and blurred the endless white sweep of the prairie. She ached in too many ways to count. It would be easier to give in to it, to let her knees crumple and drop down into the snow, let the helplessness wash over her. Snow battered her cheeks, stinging with needle sharpness. If she wanted the future she had planned, the promise of a life on her own and alone, so no one could own her or hurt her, then she must find the gelding. She must bring him in and finish the barn work. Those were her only choices.

What would her friends say? She plunged deeply into the snow, following the set of telltale tracks snaking through the deeply drifted snow. She sank past her knees, hefting her skirts, ignoring the biting cold. She imagined sitting in Lila's cozy parlor above the mercantile her parents owned with the fire crackling and steeping tea scenting the room, surrounded by those who were more family to her than her own parents.

"Fee, you ought to stay with one of us instead of leaving town," Kate might say in that stubborn, gentle way of hers. "I'm sure my folks would put you up if I told them what your home life is like."

"Or you would stay with us," Lila would offer with a look of mischief. "My stepmother would be more than happy to take you in and manage your life."

"Or with me," Earlee would say. "My family doesn't have much, but I know we could make room for you."

Fiona's throat ached with love for her friends, and she knew she could not share this with them. Some things were too painful and besides, her parents would come for her if she stayed anywhere in Angel County. The new sheriff was one of Pa's card-playing buddies. She feared for her friends. There was no telling what Pa might do if he were angry enough. It would be best to find the horse.

A plaintive neigh carried toward her on the cutting wind. Flannigan was easy to spot, standing defiantly on a rise of the prairie, a rusty splash of color in the white and gray world. Thank heavens! She faced the brutal wind. If she could get to him fast enough, she could lead him back to his stall and no one would be the wiser. The strap would remain on the lean-to wall untouched and unused. Relief slid through her and her feet felt light as she hurried on. The deep snow clutched at her boots as if with greedy hands, slowing her progress.

On the rise ahead, the gelding watched her

brashly. Now all she had to do was to hold out her hand and speak gently to him, and surely he would come to her as he did in the corral. To her surprise, the gelding tossed his head, sending another ringing neigh echoing across the landscape. He turned and ran, disappearing into the folds of land and the veil of snowfall.

No! She watched him vanish. Her hopes went with him. What if he kept running? What if she could never catch him? What if she had to return home and face Da's wrath? She plunged after him. She reached the crest where he'd stood and searched the prairie for him. Her eyes smarted from staring into the endless white. Panic clawed at the back of her neck, threatening to overtake her.

Get the horse, her instincts told her. Run after him as far as it takes. Just get him back before Da comes home. She closed out the picture of the dark lean-to and her father's harsh words as he yelled at her, listing everything she had done wrong. Desperation had her lunging down the steep rise, sobbing in great lungfuls of wintry air, searching frantically for any movement of color in the vast white.

There he was, flying through an empty

field, black mane and tail rippling, racing the wind. What would it be like to run as far and as fast as you could go, to be nothing but part of the wind, the snow and sky?

"Flannigan!" she cried out, praying that her voice carried to him. But it was not her voice that caused the giant workhorse to spin and turn toward town. A distant neigh echoed across the rolling fields and like a death toll it reverberated in her soul. Would he keep running? How would she ever catch him?

"Flannigan!"

The horse hesitated, his tail up and his black mane fluttering in the wind. Proud and free, the gelding tossed his head as if troubled, torn between galloping over to her and his own freedom.

She knew just how he felt, exactly how attractive the notion of fleeing could be. Please don't do it, she begged with all her might, but it made no difference. The gelding rocked back on his hooves and pivoted, running like a racehorse on the last stretch. She took off after him, wishing she could do the same, her skirts fluttering in the winter wind.

Ian McPherson sat up straighter on the hard wooden edge of the homemade sled's seat, trying to get a better look at the young woman in the fields. Flecks of white stung his eyes and cheeks and the storm closed in, turning serious, as if to hide her from his sight. He caught flashes of red skirt ruffles beneath the modest dove-gray coat and a mane of thick black curls flying behind her. "Who is that running through the snow?"

"If I tell you the truth, you will have a mind to get back on that train." O'Rourke was a somber man and his hard face turned grim. "We couldn't beat common sense into that girl. Don't think we didn't try."

Ian gulped, knowing his shock had to show on his face. He could find no civil response as he turned his attention back to the young lady who hiked her skirts up to her knees, showing a flash of flannel long johns before the storm and the rolling prairie stole her from view. "She's got some speed. Can't say I have seen a woman run that fast before."

"Likely her neglect is the reason the gelding got out. That girl hasn't got a lick of sense, but she *is* a good worker. My wife and I made sure of it. That's what a man needs in a helpmate. She will be useful. No need to worry about that."

"Oh, I won't." Useful. Not what he wanted

in a wife. He didn't want a wife. He had more than enough responsibility resting on his shoulders.

Aye, coming here was not the wisest decision he had ever made. But what other choice did he have? Creditors had taken his grandparents' house and land, and he still felt sick in his gut at being unable to stop it. Gaining a wife when he was near to penniless was not a good solution, even if his nana thought so. A better solution would be to find his own wife sometime in the future, even though, being a shy man, courting did not come easily to him.

"Don't make up your mind on her just yet." O'Rourke hit the gelding's flank fairly hard with his hand whip. The animal leaped forward, lathering with fear. "You come sit down to eat with us and look her over real good."

Look her over? The father spoke as if they were headed to a horse sale. Ian strained to catch another glimpse of her, but saw only gray prairie and white snow. What would the girl look like up close and face-to-face? Probably homely and pocked, considering her parents were desperate to marry her off.

"Remember, you gave us your word." O'Rourke spit tobacco juice into the snow on his side of the sled. "I don't cotton to men who go back on their word."

"I only said I would come meet the girl. I made no promises." Although he did have hopes of his own. He couldn't explain why his eyes hungrily searched for her. Maybe it was because of the pretty picture she made, like a piece from a poem, an untamed horse and the curly haired innocent chasing him. It was his imagination at work again, for he was happier in his thoughts than anywhere. Hers was an image he would pen down later tonight when he was alone with his notebook.

"Your grandfather promised." O'Rourke was like a dog with a bone. He wouldn't relent. "I knew this would happen first time you caught sight of her. Fiona is no beauty, that's for sure, but I'm strapped. Times are hard for me and my wife. We can't keep feedin' and clothin' her and we don't want to. It's high time she was married and your family and me, we had this arranged before you both was born."

He had heard it all before. Nearly the same words his grandmother had told him over and over with hope sparkling in her eyes. After all that she had lost, how could he outright disappoint her? Life was complicated and love more so.

Would the girl understand? Was she already packing her hope chest? She swept into sight, farther away, hardly more than a flash of red, a bit of gray and those bouncing black curls. From behind, she made a lovely pose, willowy and petite, with her flare of skirt and elegant outstretched hand, slowly approaching the lone horse. The animal looked lathered, his skin flicking with nervous energy as if ready to bolt again.

"Fool girl," O'Rourke growled, halting the horse near a paint-peeling, lopsided barn. "She ought to know she'll never catch the beast that way."

Her back was still to him, distant enough that she was more impression than substance, more whimsy than real with the falling snow cloaking her. If he had the time, he could capture the emotion in watercolors with muted tones and blurred lines to show her skirt and outstretched hand.

Ian vaguely realized the older man was digging in the back for something, and the rattle of a chain tore him from his thoughts and into the bitter-cold moment. He did not want to know what O'Rourke was up to; he'd seen enough of the man to expect the worst. He hopped into the deep snow, ignoring the hitch of pain in his left leg, and reached for his cane. "I shall take care of it. I have a way with horses."

"So do I." O'Rourke shook out a length of something that flickered like a snake's tongue—aye, a whip. "This won't take long with the two of us."

"No need to get yourself cold and tired out." Under no circumstances was he going to be involved in that brand of horse handling. Best to placate the man, and then figure out what he was going to do. What his grandparents hadn't told him about their best friend's son could fill a barrel. The ten-minute drive from town in the man's company was nine minutes more than he felt fit to handle. He gestured toward the ramshackle shanty up the rise a ways. "You go on up to the house where the fire is warm. Let me manage this for you."

"Well, young fellow, that sounds mighty good." O'Rourke seemed pleased and held out the whip. "I suspect you might need this."

Ian looked with distaste at the sinuous black length. "I see a rope looped over the fencepost. That will be enough."

"Suit yourself. It will be here if you need it." O'Rourke sounded amused as he tossed down the whip and sank boot-deep into the snow. He gestured toward the harnessed gelding, standing head down, as if his spirit had been broken long ago. "I'll leave this one for you to stable."

It wasn't a question, and Ian didn't like the sound of mean beneath the man's conversational tone. Still, he'd been brought up to respect his elders, so he held his tongue. O'Rourke and how he lived his life were not his concern. Seeing his grandmother through her final days and figuring out a way to make a living for both of them was his purpose.

He ought not to be giving in to his fanciful side, but with every step he took he noted the gray daylight falling at an angle, shadows hugging the lee side of rises and fence posts, but not over the girl. As he loosened the harness and lifted the horse collar from the gelding's back, he felt a strange longing, for what he did not know. Perhaps it was the haunting beauty of this place of sweeping prairies and loneliness. Maybe it was simply from traveling so long and far from everything he knew. There was another possibility, and one he didn't much want to think on.

He led the horse to the corral gate, unlooped the coiled rope from the post, used the rails to struggle onto the horse's back and swiped snow from his eyelashes.

Where had she gone? He breathed in the prairie's stillness, coiling the long driving reins and knotting them. He leaned to open the gate and directed the horse through. No animal stirred, a sign the storm setting in was bound to get worse. Only the wind's flat-noted wail chased across the rolling and falling white prairie. Different from his Kentucky home, and while he missed the trees and verdant fields, this sparse place held beauty, too.

"C'mon, boy." He drew the gate closed behind them. The crest where he'd last spotted the girl and horse was empty. He pressed the gelding into a quick walk. Falling flakes tapped with greater force and veiled the sky and the horizon, closing in on him until he could no longer see anything but gray shadows and white snow. He welcomed the beat of the wild wind and needle-sharp flakes. The farmer in him delighted in the expansive fields and the sight of a cow herd foraging in the far distance. Aye, he missed his family's homestead. He missed the life he had been born to.

When he reached the hill's crest, hoofprints and shoe prints merged and circled, clearly trailing northward. A blizzard was coming, that was his guess, for the wind became cruel and the snowflakes furious. At least he had tracks to follow. He did not want to think what he would find when he was face-to-face with the woman. He could only pray she did not want this union any more than he did. And why would she? he mused as he tucked his cane in one hand. The girl would likely want nothing to do with him, a washed-up horseman more comfortable chatting with his animals than a woman.

Perhaps it was Providence that brought the snow down like a shield, protecting him from sight as he nosed the horse into the teeth of the storm. Maybe the Almighty knew how hard it was going to be for him to face the girl, and sent the wind to swirl around him like a defense. He could do this; he drew in a long breath of wintry air and steeled his spine. Talking to a woman might not be his strong suit, but he had done more terrifying things. Right now none came to mind, but that was only because his brains muddled whenever a female was nearby. Which meant that somewhere in the thick curtain of white, Miss Fiona O'Rourke, his betrothed, had to be very close.

He heard her before he saw her. At least he *thought* that was her. The quiet soprano was sheer beauty, muted by the storm and unconsciously true, as if the singer were unaware of her gifted voice. Sure rounded notes seemed to float amid the tumbling snowflakes, the melody hardly more than a faint rise and fall until the horse drew him closer and he recognized the tune.

"O come all ye faithful," she sang. "Joyful and triumphant."

He wondered how anything so warm and sweet could be borne on the bitterest winds he'd ever felt. They sliced through his layers of wool and flannel like the sharpest blade, and yet her sweet timbre lulled him warmly, opening his heart when the cruel cold should have closed it up tight.

"O come ye, oh come ye…" The snowfall parted enough to hint at the shadow of a young woman, dark curls flecked with white, holding out her hand toward the darker silhouette of the giant draft horse. "To Bethlehem. Come and behold him…"

The horse he rode plunged toward her as if captivated. Ian understood. He, too, felt drawn to her like the snowflakes to the ground. They were helpless to take another course from sky to earth just as he could not help drawing the horse to a stop to watch. Being near to her should have made his palms sweat and cloying tightness take over his chest, but he hardly noticed his suffocating shyness. She moved like poetry with her hand out to slowly catch hold of the trembling horse.

"Born the king of angels. O come let us adore him." Her slender, mittened hand was close to touching the fraying rope halter. "O come—"

"Let us adore him." The words slipped out in his deeper baritone, surprising him.

She started, the horse shied. The bay threw his head out of her reach and with a protesting neigh, took off and merged with the snowy horizon.

"Look what you have done." Gone was the music as she swirled to face him. He expected a tongue-lashing or at the very least a bit of a scolding for frightening the runaway. But as she marched toward him through the downfall, his chin dropped and his mind emptied. Snow-frosted raven curls framed a perfect heart-shaped face. The woman had a look of sheer perfection with sculpted high cheekbones, a dainty nose and the softest mouth he'd ever seen. If she were to smile, he reckoned she could stop the snow from falling.

He took in her riotous black curls and the red gingham dress ruffle peeking from beneath her somber gray coat. Shock filled him. *"You* are Fiona O'Rourke?"

"Yes, and just who is the baboon who has chased off my da's horse and will likely cost me my supper?" She lifted her chin, setting it so that it did not look delicate at all but stubborn and porcelain steel. She looked angry, aye, but there was something compelling about Miss O'Rourke and it wasn't her unexpected beauty. Never in his life had he seen such immense sadness.

Chapter Two

Who was this strange man towering over her and what was he doing in her family's fields? Fiona swiped her eyes, trying to see the intruder more clearly. The storm enfolded him, blurring the impressive width of his powerful shoulders and casting his face in silhouette. The high, wide brim of his hat added mystery; he was surely no one she had seen on the country roads or anywhere in town. He did not seem to have a single notion of what he had just done, scaring off Flannigan again, when she'd almost had his halter in a firm grip.

"What possessed you to trespass into our fields?" She was working up a good bit of mad. Time had to be running out. She had not been watching the road well, but Da's sled might come down the road at any moment. She had no time to waste. "Why are you here?"

"I heard your singing."

"What? And you felt you had to join in the caroling?" Men. She had little use for them. Aside from her brother, she did not know a single one without some selfish plan. "Go sing somewhere else. I have a horse to catch."

"Then hop up." He held out his hand, wide palmed, the leather of his expensive driving gloves worn and thin in spots.

"Hop up? You mean ride with you?" Was the man delusional? She took a step back. Angel County was a safe, family place, but trouble wandered through every now and then on the back of a horse. The ruffian in front of her certainly looked like trouble with his quality hat, polished boots and wash-worn denims. And his horse, there was something familiar about the big bay who was reaching out toward her coat pockets as if seeking a treat.

"Riley?" Her chin dropped in shock, and she knew her mouth had to be hanging open unattractively. She could hear her parents' voices in her head. *Close your mouth, Fiona. With your sorry looks you don't want to make anything worse, for then we'll never be rid of ya.*

She snapped her jaw shut, her teeth clacking. "What are you doing on our horse?"

"I know your father" was all he said.

"My da was driving Riley. Does that mean he is back home so soon?"

"Aye." His brogue was a trace, but it sent shivers down her spine. Something familiar teased at the edges of her mind, but it wasn't stronger than the panic.

"My father is home," she repeated woodenly. "Then he must know the other work-horse has gone missing."

"Afraid so. We had a good view of you racing after the horse from the crest of the road." His hand remained outstretched. "Do you want me to catch him for you, or do you want to come?"

She withered inside. It was too late, then. She would be punished even if she brought the horse back, and if not, then who knew what would happen? This strange man's eyes were kind, shadowed as they were. Yet all she could see was a long punishment stretching out ahead of her. After the strap, she would be sent to her tiny attic room, where she would spend her time when she was not doing her share of the work. And that was *if* she brought the horse back.

If she lost Flannigan, she could not let herself imagine what her parents would do. This man had no stake in finding the horse. She did not understand why he was helping her, but her hand shot out. The storm was worsening. There wasn't a lot of time. "Take me with you."

"All right, then." He clasped her with surprising strength and swept her into the air. Her skirts billowed, the heel of her high barn boot lightly brushed Riley's flank and she landed breathlessly behind the man, her hand still in his.

"Who are you?" The storm fell like twilight, draining the gray daylight from the sky and deepening the shadows beneath the brim of his hat. She couldn't make out more than the strong cut of a square jaw, rough with a day's dark growth.

"There will be time enough for that later. Hold on tight." He drew her hand to his waist. He could have been carved marble beneath his fine wool coat. With a "get up!" Riley shot out into an abrupt trot, the bouncing gait knocking her back on the horse's rump. She slid in teeth-rattling jolts, each bump knocking her farther backward. Her skirt, indecorously around her knees, slid with her.

A leather-gloved hand reached around to grip her elbow and hold her steady. "Never ridden astride before?"

"Not without a saddle." The words flew out before she could stop them. If her parents knew she had ever ridden in such an unladylike fashion, they would tan her hide for sure. But the stranger, whoever he was, did not seem shocked by her behavior.

"Just hold on tight to me and grip the horse's sides with your knees."

Did she ask for his advice? No. Her face blushed. She might not have been bashful riding this way with her brother watching, but this man was a different matter. She fell silent, bouncing along, staring hard at the stranger's wide back. Riley's gait smoothed as he reached out into a slow canter, and she raised her face into the wind, letting the icy snow bathe her overheated skin.

Lord, please don't make me regret this. Yes, she was second-guessing her impulsive decision to ride with this man, this stranger. Maybe he was the new neighbor down the way. The Wilsons' farm had sold last month. Or maybe this was the new deputy come to town. Either way, she needed to find the horse.

"Hold up." The stranger had a resonant voice, pleasantly masculine. He leaned to the side, studying the ground. The accumulation rapidly erased Flannigan's hoofprints. "I think he's turned northwest. There's a chance we won't lose him yet."

"We can't lose him." Terror struck her harder than any blizzard.

"I'll do my best, miss. Are you sure you don't want me to turn around and take you back to your warm house?"

"You don't understand. I can't go back unless I have the horse." She shivered and not from the cold. No one understood—no one but her best friends, that was—how severe her life was. She had learned a long time ago to do her best with the hand God had dealt her. She would be eighteen and on her own soon enough. Then she would never have to be dominated by anyone. She would never have to be hurt again. "Please. We have to keep going."

"You sound desperate. That horse sure must mean something to you." Gruffly spoken, those words, although it was hard to tell with the wind's howl filling her ears. He

pressed Riley back to a canter. The storm
beat at them from the side now, brutally tearing through layers of clothes. Her hands hurt
from the cold.

Night was falling; the shadows grew darker
as the stranger stopped the horse to study the
ground again and backtracked at a slow walk.
With every step Riley took, her heart thudded
painfully against her ribs. *Please, don't let
me lose Flannigan,* she begged—prayer was
too gentle of a request. She should have been
more vigilant. She should have realized something was amiss when the horse hung back
in the corral instead of racing to the barn for
his supper. Had she been quicker, this never
would have happened. And she wouldn't be
fearing the beating to come.

You could just keep on going. The thought
came as if whispered in the wind. They were
headed away from town and toward the east-
ern road that would take her straight to Newberry, the neighboring railroad town. She
could send word to her friend Lila, who could
gather the girls and find a way to unearth her
money sock from the loose floorboard in the
haymow.

"There he is." The stranger wheeled Riley
around with a confident efficiency she had

never seen before. The huge animal followed his light commands willingly, this gelding who had lost his will to care long ago.

It was impossible to see around the broad line of the man's back. When he unlooped the rope and slip knotted it while he directed Riley with his knees, hope burrowed into her and took root. Maybe catching Flannigan would be quick and painless, if the stranger was as good with a lasso as he was with the horse.

"Hold on. He's bolting."

That was her only warning before he shouted "Ha!" and pressed Riley into a plunging gallop. Snow battered her from all directions, slapping her face. The horse's movements beneath her weren't smooth. He was fighting through the uneven snow and she jounced around, gripping the stranger's coat tightly.

"Can you stay on?" He shouted to be heard over the cadence of the horse and the roaring blizzard.

She wanted to but her knees were slipping, her skirt had blown up to expose her red flannel petticoats and long johns and she was about to slide off the downside slope of Riley's rump. "No," she called out as she slid farther. A few seconds more and there would be nothing beneath her but cold air and pounding hooves.

"I'll be back for you." To her surprise, the stranger twisted around, caught hold of her wrist and swept her safely to the side, away from the dangerous hooves. She landed in the snow on her feet, sinking in a drift past her knees. Horse and rider flew by like a dream, moving as one dark silhouette in the coming night.

Cold eked through her layers and cleaved into her flesh, but she hardly noticed. She stood transfixed by the perfect symmetry between man and horse. With manly grace he slung the lasso, circling it twice overhead before sending it slicing through the white veil. Without realizing it, she was loping through the impossible drifts after them, drawn to follow as if by an invisible rope. Perhaps it was the man's skill that astonished her as the noose pulled tight around defiant Flannigan's neck. She could not help admiring the strength it took to hold the runaway, or the dance of command and respect as the horse and rider closed the distance. A gloved hand reached out, palm up to the captive gelding. The stranger's low mumble seemed to warm the bitter air. Her brother could not have done better.

"Our runaway seems tame enough." He emerged out of the shadows, towering over her, leading Flannigan by a short lead. He dismounted, sliding effortlessly to the ground. "He got a good run in, so he ought to be in a more agreeable mood for the journey back. Let me give you a foot up."

He was taller than she realized; then again, perhaps it was because her view of him had changed. He was bigger somehow, greater for the kindness he had shown to Flannigan, catching him without a harsh word or a lash from a whip, as Da would have done. She shook her head, skirting him. "I'll ride Flannigan in. He ought to be tired enough after his run. He's not a bad horse."

"No, I can see that. Just wanted to escape his bonds for a time."

Yes. That was how she felt, too. Flannigan nickered low in his throat, a warm surrender or a greeting, she didn't know which. She irrationally hated that he had been caught. It was not safe for him to run away, for there were too many dangers that ranged from gopher holes to barbed wire to wolves, but she knew what it felt like to be trapped. When she gazed to the north where the spill and swell of land should be, she saw only the impenetrable white wall of the storm. Although the prairie had disappeared, she longed to take off and go as fast and as far as she could until she was a part of the wind and the sky.

"Then up you go." The stranger didn't argue, merely knelt at her feet and cupped his hands together. "I'm sure a beauty such as you can tame the beast."

Did she imagine a twinkle in his eyes? It was too dark to know for sure. She was airborne and climbing onto Flannigan's back before she had time to consider it. By then the stranger had limped away into the downfall, a hazed silhouette and nothing more.

You could take Flannigan and go. It was her sense of self-preservation whispering at her to flee. It felt foolish to give in to the notion of running away, right now at least; it felt even more foolish to lead the horse home. Da had fallen into an especially dark mood these last few months since he had lost much of the harvest. Thinking of the small, dark sitting room where Da would be waiting drained the strength from her limbs. She dug her fingers into Flannigan's coarse mane, letting the blizzard rage at her.

"I'll lead you." His voice came out of the thickening darkness. There was no light now, no shades of grayness or shadows to demark him. "So there will be no more running away."

Her pulse lurched to a stop. He couldn't know, she told herself. He might be able to lasso a horse, but he could not read minds. That was impossible. Still, her skin prickled as Flannigan stepped forward, presumably drawn by the rope. His gait rolled through her, and she felt boneless with hopelessness. The wind seemed to call to her as it whipped past, speeding away to places unknown and far from here, far from her father's strap.

This was December. She had to stick it out until May. Only six months more. Then she would have graduated, the first person in her family to do so. That meant something to her, an accomplishment that her parents would never understand, but her closest friends did. An education was something no one could take from her. It was something she could earn, although she did not have fine things the way Lila's family did, or attend an East Coast finishing school as Meredith was doing. An education was something she could take with her when she left; her love of books and learning would serve her well wherever she went and whatever job she found.

It will be worth staying, she insisted, swiping snow from her eyes. Although her heart and her spirit ached for her freedom and the dream of a better, gentler life, she stayed on Flannigan's broad back. His lumbering gait felt sad and defeated, and she bowed her head, fighting her own sorrow.

"I know how you feel, big guy." Going home to a place that wasn't really a home. She patted one mostly numb hand against his neck and leaned close until his mane tickled her cheek. "I almost have enough money saved up. When I leave, I can keep some of it behind for payment and take you. How would you like to ride in a boxcar? Let's just think of what it will be like to ride the rails west."

Flannigan nickered low in his throat, a comforting sound, as if he understood far more than an animal should. She stretched out and wrapped her arms around his neck as far as they could reach and held on. Come what may, at least Flannigan would not be punished. She would see to that. She would take full responsibility for his escape.

And what about the stranger? She couldn't see any sign of him except for the tug of the rope leading Flannigan inexorably forward. There was no hint of the stranger's form in the gloom until they passed through the corral gate and she caught the faintest outline of him ambling through the snow to secure the latch. Flannigan blew out a breath, perhaps a protest at being home again. She drew her leg over the horse's withers and straightened her skirt.

"I'll help you." His baritone surprised her and he caught her just as she started to slide. Against her will, she noticed the strength in his arms as she was eased to the ground. She sank deep and unevenly into a drift. His helpfulness didn't stop. "Can you find your way to the house, or should I take you there?"

"I have to see to the horses."

"No, that's what I plan to do. Let me get them sheltered in the barn and then I'll be seeing you safely in." Stubbornness rang like a note in his rumbling voice.

She had a stubborn streak, too. "I'm hardly used to taking orders from a stranger. These are not your horses, and what are you doing on this land?"

"Your da invited me."

"A drinking buddy, no doubt. It must be poker night already." She shook her head, plowing through the uncertain drifts and trailing her mittens along Flannigan's neck until she felt the icy rope. She curled her fingers around it, holding on tight. "I don't allow intoxicated strangers to handle my horses."

"Intoxicated?" He chuckled at that. "Missy, I'm parched. I won't deny, though, I could use a drink when I'm through."

Was that a hint of humor she heard in his lilting brogue? Was he teasing her? He had a gentle hand when it came to horses, but he could be the worst sort of man; any friend of her father's would be. Birds of a feather. She saw nothing funny about men like her da. She pushed past him, knocking against the iron plane of his chest with her shoulder.

"Go up to the house, then, and you can wet your whistle, as my da would say." Why was she so disappointed? It wasn't as if she cared anything about this man. She didn't even know his name. It just went to show that men could not be trusted, even if they were prone to good deeds.

"That's it? I help you bring in your horse and now you are banishing me from your barn?"

"Yes." Why was he sounding so amused? A decent man ought to have some semblance of shame. "Likely as not, my da already has the whiskey poured and waiting for you."

"Then he'll be a mite disappointed." The stranger grasped the rope she held, taking charge of Flannigan. "Come along. The barn is not far, if I remember, although I cannot see a foot in front of me."

"Just follow the fence line." She was tugged along when she ought to stand her ground. There was something intriguing about this stranger. It was not like one of Da's fellows to choose barn work over cheap whiskey.

"This is better." She heard his words as if from a great distance, but that was the distortion of the wind and the effort as he heaved open the barn door. She realized she was the only one gripping Flannigan's rope and held him tightly, leading him into the dark shelter of the main aisle.

"Where is the lantern?" His boots padded behind her, leading Riley into the barn.

"I was just getting to that." Really. As if she expected them all to stand around in the dark. She wrestled off her mittens, ice tinkling to the hard-packed dirt at her feet, and felt with numb fingertips for the match tin.

"Need any help?"

"No." Her hands were not cooperating.

She balled them up and blew on them, but her warm breath was not enough to create any thaw. She must be colder than she thought. Boots padded in her direction, sure and steady in spite of the inky blackness. Although she could not see him, she could sense him. The scent of soap and clean male skin and melting snow. The rustle of denim and wool. His masculine presence radiating through the bitter air.

The shock of his touch jolted through her. She stumbled backward, but he held her hands, warming them with his. The act was so unexpected and intimate, shock muted her. Her mouth opened, but not a single sound emerged. He was as if a part of the darkness but his touch was warm as life and somehow not threatening—when it should be.

We're alone, she realized, her pulse quickening. Alone in the dark, in the storm and with a strange man. She felt every inch of the yawning emptiness around her, but not fear. Her hands began to warm, tucked safely within his. She wanted to pull away and put proper distance between them, but her feet forgot how to move. She forgot how to breathe.

"There. You are more than a wee bit chilly.

You need better mittens." He broke the hold first, his voice smooth and friendly, as if unaffected by their closeness. "Now that my eyes are used to the dark, I can almost see what I'm doing."

Her hearing registered the scrape of the metal match tin against the wooden shelf on the post, the strike of the match and Flannigan's heavy step as he nosed in behind her. Light flared to life, a sudden shock in the blackness, and the caress of it illuminated a rock-solid jawline and distinctive planes of a man's chiseled, rugged face.

A young man's face. Five o'clock shadow hugged his jaw and a faint smile softened the hard line of his sculpted mouth. He had to be twenty at the oldest. As he touched the flame to the lantern wick, the light brightened and highlighted the dependable line of his shoulders and the power of his muscled arms. A man used to hard work. Not one of Da's friends, then, or at least not one she had seen before.

"How do you know my father?" Her voice scraped along the inside of her throat, sounding as raw as it felt.

"I don't." He shrugged his magnificent shoulders simply, an honest gesture. He shook out the match and stowed it carefully in the bottom drawer of the lantern's base. "I never met him until this day, although I grew up hearing tales about him and my father. And I know who you are, Fiona O'Rourke."

A terrible roaring filled her ears, louder than the blizzard's wail, louder than any sound she had ever known. The force of it trembled through her, and she felt as if a lasso were tightening around her neck. Her dreams cracked apart like breaking ice. "Y-you know me?"

"Aye." Gently came that single word.

"But how? Unless you are—" Her tongue froze, her mind rolled around uselessly because she knew exactly who he was. For she had grown up hearing those same tales of her da and another man, the man whose son now towered before her. "No, it can't be."

"Ian McPherson. Your betrothed." Since the lantern was lit, he seized a cane that she now noticed leaning against the post. He leaned on it, walking with a limp to snare Flannigan's lead rope. "Come, big fellow. I'll get you rubbed down. That's a fine coat of lather you have there."

Ian McPherson. Here? The ground beneath her boots swayed, and she gripped a nearby stall door. For as long as she could remember, Ma and Da would talk of better times when they were young and of their friends the McPhersons. Sometimes they would mention the old promise between older friends that their children would one day marry. But that was merely an expectation, a once-made wish and nothing more. Whatever her parents might think, *she* was certainly not betrothed and certainly not to a stranger.

The barn door crashed open, startling the horses. Flannigan, now cross tied in the aisle, threw his head and tried to bolt, but the lines held him fast. Riley, who was not tied, rocked back onto his hindquarters, wheeled in the breezeway and took off in a blind run.

Da grabbed the reins, yanking down hard enough to stop the gelding in his tracks. The horse's cry of pain sliced through her shock and she raced to Riley's side. Her hands closed around the reins, trying to work them from her father's rough hands.

"I'll take him, Da. He needs to be rubbed down—"

"McPherson will do it." His anger roared above the storm. "No need to see how the gelding got loose. You nearly lost the second one, fool girl. If I hadn't been standing here to stop him, he would have gotten out. Come to the house."

Fiona wasn't surprised when he released his iron hold on the reins to clamp his bruising fists around her upper arms and escort her to the door.

"McPherson, you come on up when you're done. Maeve has a hot supper ready and waiting."

Fiona heard the low resonance of Ian's answer but not his words. The hurling wind beating against her stole them away, and she felt more alone than ever as she was tugged like a captive along the fence line toward the house. Her father muttered angrily at the storm and at her, promising to teach her a lesson. She blocked out images of the punishment she knew was to come, her feet heavy and wooden. As Da jerked her furiously along, the wide, endless prairie, hidden in the storm, seemed to call to her. She stumbled but did not fall.

Chapter Three

The lean-to was black, without a single flicker of light. Da's boots pounded like rapid gunshots across the board floor, the sound drowning out her lighter step. The sharp scent of coal in the far corner greeted her as the door slammed shut behind her with a resounding crack. Even the blizzard was angrier, beating at the closed door with immeasurable fury.

At least she was numb now. She had tucked her feelings deep so that nothing could really hurt her. The inky darkness made it easier. She heard Da's steps silence. The rasp of leather as he yanked the strap from the nail came louder than the raging storm.

"You're darn lucky that McPherson hasn't changed his mind outright and hightailed it back to Kentucky." Low and soft, her father's voice was deceptively calm as he ambled close.

Although she could not see him, she sensed his nearness as easily as she sensed the strap he clutched in both hands. "You didn't tell me he was coming."

"Doesn't matter if you know or you don't. You will marry him."

"But why?" She choked against the panic rising like bile in her throat. Her instincts shouted at her to step back and run. The door wasn't far. A few quick steps and she would be lost in the storm. Da couldn't catch her, not if she ran with all her might.

But how far would she get? The storm was turning deadly, with the temperature well below zero. Even if she could make it to Earlee's house, her friend lived more than half a mile away. She would freeze if she tried to walk that far.

"It's not your place to ask questions, missy." Da grabbed her roughly by the shoulder and shoved her. "It's your place to do what yer told."

Knocked off balance, Fiona shot her hands out, but she couldn't see the wall. Her knuckles struck wood and she landed hard against the boards. She hardly felt the jolting pain, because it wasn't going to be anything compared to what was coming.

"Let me tell you what, girl." Da worked himself into a higher rage, smacking the strap against his gloved palm. "If McPherson changes his mind and won't have you, you'll be the one to pay. I'll make this look like a Sunday picnic—"

She gritted her teeth and closed her eyes, breathing slowly in and slowly out, ready for the bite of the strap. She heard the rustle of clothing, imagining her father was drawing his arm back for the first powerful blow. This won't be so bad, she told herself, gathering what strength she had. She could endure this as she had many times before. She braced herself for the worst. It was best if she thought of being elsewhere, maybe astride Flannigan galloping toward the horizon. She imagined the strike of snow on her face and freedom filling her up. If only she could ignore the hissing strap as it flew downward toward her.

The lean-to door burst open with a thundering crack, and the strap never touched her back. Footsteps hammered on the board floor and Da cursed. Her eyes had adjusted enough to make out the shadowed line of two upraised arms, as if locked in battle. But the taller man, the stronger man, took the strap in hand and stepped away.

"It's over, O'Rourke," Ian McPherson's baritone boomed like an avalanche. "You won't beat this girl again. You hear me?"

"This is my house. You have no call giving me orders."

"If you want me to consider marrying the girl, I do." Warm steel, those words, and coldly spoken. He unwound the strap from where it had wrapped around his hand. Had he caught it in midstrike? Was he hurt?

It was hard to think past the relief rolling through her and harder to hear her thoughts over her father's mumbled anger. He was saying something, words she couldn't grasp, while Ian stood his ground, feet braced, stance unyielding. His words echoed in her hollow-feeling skull. *If you want me to consider marrying the girl…*

She squeezed her eyes shut. *Marry.* She wasn't yet eighteen; her birthday was nearly five months away. The last thing she wished to do with her life was to trust a man with it.

"What is going on out here?" Ma's sharp tone broke through whatever the men were discussing. Fiona opened her eyes, blinking against the stinging brightness as lamplight tumbled into the lean-to, glazing the man with blood staining his glove.

"Just setting a few things straight with the boy." Da pounded past her. "Don't stand there gawkin', woman. Get me a drink."

The door closed partway, letting in enough light to see the tension in his jaw. Ian McPherson hung the strap on the nail where it belonged, his shoulders rigid, his back taut. She inched toward the door, torn between being alone with an angry man and feeling responsible for his bleeding hand. He'd caught the strap, taking the blow meant for her.

Warmth crept around her heart, but it couldn't be something like admiration. No, she would not allow any soft or tender feelings toward the man who wanted to bridle her in matrimony. She would be less free than she was now; this she knew from her mother's life. Still, no one aside from Johnny had ever stood up for her. It wasn't as if she could leave Ian McPherson bleeding alone in the dark.

"Is it deep?" She was moving toward him without a conscious decision to do so; she reached out to cradle his hand in her own. Blood seeped liberally from the deep gash in his leather glove. It had been a hard strike, then, if the strap had sliced through the material easily. She swallowed hard, hating to think that he was badly cut.

"I believe I shall live." Although the tension remained in his jaw and tight in his powerful muscles, his voice was soft, almost smiling. "I've been hurt much worse than this."

"If you have, then it wasn't on my behalf." She gingerly peeled off his glove, careful of the wound, which looked much worse once she could clearly see it. Her stomach winced in sympathy. She knew exactly how much that hurt. "Come into the kitchen so I can clean this properly."

"I left the horses standing, and that's not good for them in this cold." He withdrew his hand from hers, although slowly and as if with regret. "I'll bandage it myself when the horses are comfortable."

"This should not wait." Men. Even Johnny had been the same, oblivious to common sense when it came to cuts and illnesses. "You need stitches, and you cannot do that on your own."

"I might surprise you. I have some skill with a needle."

"Now you are teasing me." She caught the upturned corners of his mouth. He wasn't grinning, but the hint of it drew her and she smiled in spite of her objections to the man. "I'm not going to like you. I think it's only fair that I give you honest warning."

"I appreciate that." He didn't seem offended as he pulled away and punched through the door, holding it open to the pummeling snow. "It's only fair to tell you that I don't dislike you nearly as much as I expected to, Fiona O'Rourke. Now, stay in the house where it's warm. I'll be back soon enough and you can minister to my cut to your heart's content."

The shadows did not seem to cling to her with their sadness as he offered her one lingering look, and reassurance washed over her. She could not explain why she felt safe in a way she never had before; nothing had changed. Not one thing. Da was still drinking in the kitchen, Ma was still worn and irritable with unhappiness and exhaustion as salt pork sizzled in a fry pan, and yet the lamplight seemed brighter as she followed it through the door and into the kitchen where more work awaited her.

He had not bargained on feeling sorry for the girl and bad for her plight. Ian took a drink of hot tea, uncomfortable with the tension surrounding him. Other than the clink of steel forks on the serviceable ironware plates, there was no other sound. Mrs. O'Rourke, a faded woman with sharp angles and a sallow face, kept her head down and shoveled up small bites of baked beans, fried potatoes and salt pork with uninterrupted regularity. Mr. O'Rourke was hardly different, his persistent frown deepening the angles of his sharp features.

These were not happy nor prosperous people. What had happened to the family over the years? What hardships? While it wasn't his business, he was curious. This was not the wealthy family from his grandparents' stories. Not sure what to say, he kept silent and broke apart a sourdough biscuit to butter it. Searing pain cut through his hand. He'd used a strip of cloth as a bandage, but judging by the looks of things the cut was still bleeding. He would worry about it later. His mind was burdened, and he had greater concerns.

A single light flickered in the nearby wall lamp, but it was not strong enough to reach beyond the circle of the small table. He'd caught a glimpse of the kitchen when he'd come in from the barn, but Mrs. O'Rourke had been in the process of carrying the food from the stove to the table in the corner of the spare, board-sided room. A ragged curtain hung over a small window, the ruffle sagging with neglect. The furniture was spare and decades old, battered and hardly more than serviceable. Judging by the outline of the shack he'd seen through the storm, the dwelling was in poor repair and housed three tiny rooms, maybe four.

Nana is never going to believe this, he thought as he set down his cup. What happened to the O'Rourke family's wealth? Times looked as if they had always been hard here. His chest tightened. He had some sympathy for that. Recent hardships had broken his family. But he reckoned in the old days when they had all been sitting around the peat fire dreaming of the future, his grandparents could not have foreseen this. There was no fortune here to save the McPherson family reputation. His grandmother was going to be devastated.

"More beans?" O'Rourke grunted from the head of the table, holding the bowl that had barely one serving remaining.

Ian shook his head and took a bite of the biscuit, his troubles deepening. What of the marriage bargain made long ago, in happier times? How binding was it? It was clear the O'Rourkes wanted their daughter married. But what did Fiona want? Not marriage, by the way she was avoiding any evidence of his existence. She stared at her plate, picking at her food, looking as if in her mind she were a hundred miles away. Her features were stone, her personality veiled.

His fingers itched to sketch her. To capture the way the light tumbled across her, highlighting the dip and fall of her ebony locks and her delicate face. She could have been sculpted from ivory, her skin was so perfect. The set of her pure blue eyes and the slope of her nose and the cut of her chin were sheer beauty. There was something about her that would be harder to capture on the page, something of spirit and heart that was lovelier yet.

"I see you've taken a shine to the girl." O'Rourke sounded smug as he slurped at his coffee, liberally laced with whiskey by the smell of it. "Maeve, fetch us some of that gingerbread you made special. Fiona, get off your backside and clear this table right now. Come with me, McPherson. Feel like a card game?"

"I don't gamble." He pushed away from the table, thankful the meal had finally ended.

The floor looked unswept beneath his feet, the boards scarred and scraped.

"Didn't figure you for the type, although that grandmother of yours was a high and mighty woman." O'Rourke didn't seem as if he realized he was being offensive as he un-hooked the lamp from the wall sconce and pounded through the shadowed kitchen, carrying the light with him. "Your old man knew how to raise a ruckus. The times we had when we were young."

O'Rourke fell to reminiscing and in the quiet, Ian hesitated at the doorway, glancing over his shoulder at the young woman bent to her task at the table. New light flared in the corner—the mother had lit another lamp—and in the brightness she was once again the lyrical beauty he had seen on the prairie try-ing to tame the giant horse. He realized there was something within Fiona O'Rourke that could not be beaten or broken. Something that made awareness tug within him, like recog-nizing like.

"McPherson, are you comin'?" The bite of impatience was hard to miss, echoing along the vacant board walls.

Ian tore his gaze away, trying hard not to notice the shabby sitting room. A stove had gone cold in the corner and the older man didn't move to light a fire, probably to save the expense of coal. He set the lamp on a shelf, bringing things into better focus. Ian noted a pair of rocking chairs by the curtained window with two sewing baskets within reach on the floor. A braided gingham rug tried to add cheer to the dismal room, where two larger wooden chairs and a small, round end table were the only other furniture. He took the available chair, settling uncertainly on the cheerful gingham cushion.

"You've met Fiona, and you like what you see. Don't try to tell me you don't." O'Rourke uncapped his whiskey bottle, his gaze penetrating and sly. "Do we have a deal?"

"A deal?" Hard to say which instinct shouted more loudly at him, the one urging him to run or the one wanting to save her. Unhappiness filled the house like the cold creeping in through the badly sealed board wall. He fidgeted, not sure what to do. His grandmother would want him to say yes, but he had only agreed to come. His interest, if any, was in the land and that was hard to see buried beneath deep snowdrifts. Still, he could imagine it. The rolling fields, green come May, dotted with the small band of brood mares he had managed to hold on to. "Shouldn't we start negotiating before we agree to a deal?"

"No need." A sly grin slunk across his face, layered in mean. "Your grandmother and me, we've already come to terms. Ain't that why you're here?"

Warning flashed through him. "You and my grandmother have been in contact?"

"Why else would you be here?"

Oh, Nana. Betrayal hit him like a mallet dead center in his chest. Had his grandmother gone behind his back? "What agreement did the two of you reach?"

"Six hundred dollars. My wife and I stay in our house for as long as we live. Now, I can see by the look on your face you think that's a steep price. I won't lie to ya. The girl is a burden, but like I said, she's a hard worker. That's worth something. Besides, I saw you looking her over. A man your age needs a wife. I ought to know. That's why I settled down."

Horror filled him; he couldn't say what bothered him more. He launched out of his chair, no longer able to sit still. He thought of his frail grandmother, a woman who had lost everything she once loved. Her words warbled through his mind. *It won't hurt a thing for you to go take a look. The land might be just what we need—what you need—to start over and keep your grandfather's legacy living on.*

Legacy? That word stood out to him now. At the time, the plea on his grandmother's button face had persuaded him to come, that and the doctor's dim prognosis. Nana's heart was failing. So, he'd reasoned, how could he disappoint her in this final request? Not the marriage agreement—he had been clear with her on that—but in taking a look and in agreeing to meet the people once so important to their family.

Now, all he saw were broken dreams—his grandmother's, his grandfather's and his hopes to start again.

"What are you up to, young man?" O'Rourke slammed his bottle onto the unsteady table—not so hard as to spill the liquor—and bounded to his feet. "Your family agreed to this. The girl and six hundred dollars *and not a penny less.*"

"Six hundred for the girl?" Ian raked his good hand through his hair, struggling with what to say. The truth would probably make the man even more irate and if that happened, would he take it out on Fiona? He thought of his return ticket on tomorrow's eastbound train and shivered. His palm burned with pain, a reminder of how hard O'Rourke had meant to thrash his daughter. His stomach soured.

"I feared this would happen. She's no prize, I grant you that. I'm sorry you had to see how she can be. She could have lost that horse, and that ain't the first time she's done something like that. Trouble follows that girl, but she can be taught to pay better attention. I'll see to it."

He felt the back of his neck prickle. He glanced over his shoulder and noticed the shadow just inside the doorway to the kitchen. A glimpse of red gingham ruffle swirled out of view. She had come to listen in, had she? And what did she think of her father trying to sell her off like an unwanted horse?

"It costs to feed her and shelter her. Her ma and I are tired of the expense. Since we lost our Johnny, we don't have anyone to work the fields in the summer or in town for wages in winter."

And that's what a child was to these people? A way to earn money without working for it? "I don't have six hundred dollars, Mr. O'Rourke. My grandmother is ill and she isn't aware of how precarious our finances are. My grandfather made some bad investments. We are nearly penniless as a result."

"You have no money?" Fury rolled through the man, furrowing his leathery face and fisting his hands.

"Not a spare six hundred dollars. I didn't come to renegotiate for the girl." He had hoped he could bargain for the land with the little savings he had left. He had traveled here with a hope that O'Rourke would be willing to sell at a bargain to his friend's son. That a wedding would not have to be part of the deal.

"If you don't have the money, then this is a waste." O'Rourke cackled, the fury draining, but the bitterness growing. "Tell your grandmother the arrangement is off."

"That's for the best." Ian heard the smallest sigh of relief from behind the shadowed doorway. Again he caught sight of a flash of red gingham as she swirled away, perhaps returning to the kitchen work awaiting her. Disappointment settled deep within him. He told himself it was from losing out on land he had hoped to afford, but in truth, he could not be sure.

Chapter Four

Ma turned down the wick to save kerosene, and the small orange flicker turned the kitchen to dancing shadows. Darkness crept in from the corners of the room like the winter's cold. "Don't forget to wipe down, Fiona, after you throw out the dishwater."

"Yes, Ma." She dried her hands on the dish towel and hung it on the wall behind the stove to dry. Tiny tremors rippled through her, as they had been doing for the last half hour or so, ever since she'd heard her da's fateful words. *Tell your grandmother the arrangement is off.*

Thank the heavens. Gratitude and relief pounded through her. A terrible fate avoided, and she was grateful to God for it. As she unhooked her coat from the wall peg by the door, she caught sight of her mother pouring a cup of tea in the diminished light at the stove, her one luxury. She worked with great care to stir in a frugal amount of honey. Fiona winced, turning away from the sight, fighting pity she didn't want to feel. She herself had narrowly missed that kind of fate although her feet remained heavy as she slipped into her coat and hefted the basin of dirty wash water from the table. How could her parents do such a thing? And why? With the way Da was asking for six hundred dollars, she might as well be livestock up for sale.

Angry tears burned behind her eyes as she buttoned her coat, blurring the image of her ma's threadbare calico dress and apron, of her too-lean frame as she took a first soothing sip of tea. Fiona didn't have to look to know exhaustion hollowed her mother's face. That she would spend the rest of the evening sewing quietly with her head down while Da ranted and raved about their troubles.

Tiredly, she trudged through the lean-to and, sure enough, her father's voice followed her.

"You get that look off your face, woman." Da's shout rang too loud and slurry. "You keep that up and you'll be living in the back of a wagon. Is that what you want?"

"I didn't mean anything by it—"

"I don't care what you mean. I thought that boy had money. His family was richer than Midas. What in blazes did they squander it on? We have need of it, and that pipsqueak shows up whining about being broke. Time to get back the money we put into that girl, if you ask me. If McPherson won't take her, there's others who will."

And just who would that be? She stumbled into the brunt of the storm. The blizzard had grown, beating at her as if with enraged fists, her face full of ice so that she couldn't breathe. Her father wasn't making any sense, as usual. But he did sound determined to find a husband for her, someone who could hand over money to them. How could they do this to her? Could they actually force her to marry? No, this was America, not the homeland. It was modern times, not 1700.

But that was no comfort, none at all. The storm seemed to cage her in, blocking out the entire world. As if drowning, she knelt and upended the basin, letting the hot water steam and spill safely away from the pathway. She had underestimated her father's callousness again. Ever since Johnny's death, she had taken over all the chores Johnny used to do. His criticism had become unrelenting, and now he expected her to marry just so he could get some gain from it? She thought of her money sock tucked safely away, the savings she had set aside one coin at a time that no one knew about. Not even Johnny had known.

"Still at work?" The rugged baritone startled her.

She dropped the basin, shocked, as the hammering storm diminished. An unmistakable shadow appeared, standing between her and the fierce gusts, towering above her like righteousness. Ian McPherson.

"I couldn't hear you because of the storm." She straightened on unsteady legs. She felt beaten and battered. Did she have to face this man now, when she felt ready to crack apart? "What are you doing out here? Shouldn't you be in with my father trying to barter him down to a better price?"

"You're angry with me."

"You're smarter than you look, McPherson." Anger was easier. It was the only thing keeping her strong. She swiped annoying amounts of snow from her lashes and squinted. Yes, that was a pack slung over his left shoulder. "Why aren't you inside with a whiskey bottle? Or are you on your way to buy another bride?"

"No, not tonight. Maybe tomorrow when the storm breaks." He knelt and retrieved the basin. Night and shadow shielded him and his voice was layered, too. She could not be sure, but maybe a hint of dimples teased at the corners of his mouth. "Sorry. I see this is no joking matter."

"To you, maybe. I don't know how anyone could think—" She stopped, biting her bottom lip. This had to be a nightmare, a bad dream she would wake from at any moment, wipe the sweat from her brow and thank the heavens above it was just a dream. But it wasn't. The cruel wind gusted, chilling through her layers of wool and flannel, and she shivered, hard. Her teeth chattered. "Just get away from me, McPherson. I'm not fooled by you any longer."

"I am sorry." He lumbered close, gripping his cane tightly as he leaned on it. He remained straight and strong. "I didn't come here to hurt you."

"I'm not hurt." Devastated. Betrayed. Disillusioned. Sure, she was all of those things. She knew her parents were not the best of people, but never had she believed they would bend this low. "I'm perfectly fine."

"You're lying more than a wee bit." His leather gloves brushed her brow. His thumb rasped across her lashes, wiping away the snow because it could not be tears.

She reared away from his touch, pulse thumping as if with fear. It was too dark to see the expression on his granite face. She snatched the basin from him. "Just get going. Go on. Town is that way. Just follow the fences."

"Eager to be rid of me?"

"More than you can guess."

"I cannot blame you for that." His hand fell to her shoulder, his baritone dipping low with regret. "You're freezing out here. Let's get you back in the house."

"No, I can't go there." She thought of the four walls closing in on her and the darkness pounding with the blizzard's wail. Her ma would not look at her, and her da, if she were lucky, might already be deeply drunk with his feet up on a stool. They would be sitting here as they did every evening, as if everything were the same as it always had been.

But it wasn't. She could not stomach the notion of looking at them, or of knowing how wrong about them she had been. Sure, they were strict and often harsh. But deep down she had never thought they were this cold. She could not step foot in the sitting room, knowing what she was to them.

"You cannot be staying out here, pretty girl." Well-meaning, he shielded her from the brunt of the wind as he steered her toward the fence line. The wooden posts were nearly buried, but offered dark bobbing buoys to follow in the strange, pearled darkness.

He was taking her to the barn. Her knees went weak with relief. She turned her back on the house, gripped her skirts and followed his tall shadow through the drifts. Snow needled her face, crept down her collar and over the tops of her shoes. The prairie was out there, still and waiting, calling like an old friend. Did she listen to it? Should she set aside her hopes to finish school and leave while she could?

"Careful. It's deeper here." Nothing but a shadow ahead of her blocking the worst of the storm, Ian stopped to reach back and take her elbow. Shadow became flesh and bone, and a stranger's compassion softness in the brutal night. His grip was firm, a band of strength holding her as she struggled to lift her boot high enough to step out of the impossible drift. Her boot scraped over the berm of snow and then it was like falling, trying to find where the earth began. She went down and Ian held her safely until her toe hit ice and she found her balance.

"Want to head back?" he asked, releasing her.

The thought of being in the sitting room made her throat burn. She shook her head, letting him lead her through the darkness, and shivered deep inside, where no cold wind could possibly touch her. The image of her mother bending quietly to her task of stirring a drop of honey into her tea became all that she could see.

What if her parents thought they could pressure her to marry? Already they pressured her into doing so much. A good daughter would do more for her parents. A Christian girl would honor her parents with her obedience. Only a selfish girl would think of her own future when her family was running out of money for food and coal. Like they always did, would they talk at her and team up and make her feel as if helping them by marrying was the only right thing to do? She could hear their voices as if part of the brutal wind, chipping away at her like water against rock until she thought they might be right.

But this? Marrying a stranger against her wishes? How could that ever be right? She let the strong grip on her arm keep her upright, forcing her legs to keep moving and her feet to lift and fall into the unbearably cold snow. If her parents had their way, she could imagine her life twenty years from now: worn down by hardship and thankless work and hardened by a harsh marriage to a joyless man. That wasn't the future she wanted. That wasn't the way she wanted to live.

"Fiona?" Ian's rough voice brought her back, straining as he fought the powerful wind to hold open the barn door. He was waiting for her, a kind presence on a heartless night.

"Sorry." She stumbled across the threshold, passing so close to him she could feel the warmth of his breath. Tiny shivers skidded down her spine, from closeness or warning, she didn't know which.

"You have a lot on your mind, lass." The door banged shut, echoing in the dark.

"I wish I didn't." What she wanted was to go back to believing her future was bright. She wanted to turn back time and start over the day, armed with answers she did not now have. She knew her parents were hurting financially, but with every step she took all she could hear was her father's words. *If McPherson won't take her, there's others who will.*

"I know the feeling." His kindness could drive the cold from the air and the hopelessness from the night. Heaven help her, for she could turn toward him in the inky blackness as if she saw him. The thud of his rucksack hitting the ground and the pad of his uneven gait only confirmed it. His hand found her shoulder. "It's a tough night you've been having. Let's get you dry and warm. Come with me."

"I can take care of myself." Her deepest instinct was to push him away, to shrug off his comforting touch and turn away from his offer of help. Except for her friends, whom she trusted, she was wary of help from others, for there was always a price that came with it.

"Aye, I'm sure of it, but tonight you are heart weary. Let me help." The smoky layers of his voice could charm away the winter. His fingers brushed her chin, tugging at the hood ties until they came free. Bits of snow rained off the edge, but before they could hit her in the face, he brushed them away, every one, as if he could see them quite clearly. "You, Miss Fiona, are in worse straits than I have ever seen."

"I know. My father said—" She squeezed her eyes shut, unable to speak aloud the horrible words. "Why are they doing this? Why now?"

"Your teeth are chattering." He eased down her hood and knocked the driven ice from around her collar. "There are blankets in the corner. Come with me."

"Are you still considering marrying me?" She stood her ground.

"Not anymore." The full truth, he couldn't deny it. From the moment he had spotted her in the fields looking like snow-speckled poetry, he had been drawn. He didn't want to admit it, but something had changed. Maybe it wasn't anything more serious than pity for the girl—there was certainly a lot to feel sorry about in her circumstances—but he knew his awareness of her was not that simple. His eyes had adjusted to the darkness and he could see her wide, honest eyes, the cute slope of her nose and the new sadness on her face that tonight's events had drawn. "I came here hoping you would feel the same as I did about our betrothal."

She turned away. Her hair tumbled like a curtain shielding her from his view, but he could sense her smile, small and thoughtful and pure relief. He was able to herd her down the main aisle. The runaway horse stretched his neck over his stall gate and nickered in greeting.

"Hello, handsome." She stopped with a spin of her skirts and a stubborn set to her jaw. Tension tightened the muscles of her shoulder beneath his gloved hand, and he let her go. She breezed away from him, ice crackling in her clothing, a lithe shadow that was like a spring breeze moving through him.

Just ignore it. The feelings are bound to go away. He set his teeth on edge, tucked his cane against the post and lifted the match tin off the ledge. He needed a moment, that was all, and the feelings would pass. At least, he prayed they would pass.

"You are such a good man." Her quiet praise made the horse nicker and the other animals peer around their gates to call out for her attention. A meow rang from the rafters above. Sure enough, a black-faced cat crept into the shadows, eyes shining, to preen for the girl below.

"Mally, where have you been? I haven't

seen you all day." Her greeting made the feline purr and the cow moo plaintively, as if anxious for Fiona's attention, too.

The emotions stirred within him like embers coming to life in a hopeless place. He struck the match and lit the wick, unable to keep his gaze from following her as she reached up to touch the cat's paw. The feline's purr grew rusty as he batted at her playfully.

His fingers itched to capture this image, the Cinderella girl with her patched clothes and her Midas heart. Everything she touched seemed to love her. The cow leaned into her touch with a sigh, and the other gelding— the one he had ridden earlier—leaned so far over his stall that he cut off his air supply and began to choke.

"Riley, you poor guy. I won't forget you." She unwrapped her arms from the gelding's neck and the lantern light found her, highlighting the curve of her face, gleaming on her ebony locks and revealing her gentle nature.

He grabbed his cane and followed his shadow down the aisle. The melody of her voice trailed after him. He was not surprised when the cat bounded along the wooden beam overhead, hopped onto the grain barrel and plopped to the ground. Hurrying for more of Fiona's affection, no doubt.

Ice spiked into his skin and crept in fragments beneath his collar, but he ignored the cold and discomfort. He gathered a patched wool blanket from the end stall, where it sat on top of an equally old quilt, and stepped around the pillow and the small sewing basket tucked in the soft hay. He had spotted this private corner when he had been rubbing down the horses before supper.

"Let's get this around you before you freeze." He shook the folds from the blanket.

"Oh, I can take care of myself." Her chin came up and her eyes squinted, as if she were trying to judge his motives.

"I don't doubt that, lass, but let me." He swept close to her, near enough to breathe in the softness of her hair. She smelled like roses and dawn and fresh snow. He swallowed hard, ignoring a few more unexamined feelings that gathered within him. Emotions that felt far too tender to trust. He stepped around the cat rubbing against her ankles to drape the blanket around her shoulders. Tender it was, to tuck the wool against her collar so that she would be warmer. "I have an unexplainable need to take care of others."

"A terrible flaw." Amusement crept into the corners of her mouth, adding layers of beauty.

He felt sucker punched. Air caught in his chest, and his hand was already reaching before he realized what he was doing. His fingers brushed the curve of her cheek, soft as a spring blossom. Her black hair felt like fine silk against his knuckles. Shyness welled up, stealing all his words. It was too late to pretend he didn't care and that he could simply walk away without a backward glance come morning.

"How is your hand?" Her fingers caught his wrist, and it was like being held captive by a butterfly. Now he knew how runaway Flannigan had felt, forced to choose between Fiona and his freedom.

"It's been better." His voice caught in his throat, sounding thick and raw. He ought to step away now, put a proper distance between them and keep it that way. Best to remember he had not come here to get sweet on Fiona O'Rourke.

"Are you trying to go back on your promise?" Humor tucked into the corners of her pretty mouth.

Captivated, he could only nod. Then, realizing he had meant to shake his head, gave a half shrug.

"Too bad, McPherson. You will do as I say or pay the consequences." She tugged him across the aisle with the wash basin in one hand and the blanket cloaking her like a royal robe. "You promised I could doctor your cut to my heart's content, and I fully intend to. You need a stitch or two."

"It'll be well enough with a cleaning and a bandage," he croaked in protest. Perhaps she didn't notice the croaking or, worse, the bashfulness heating his face.

"So you're a tough guy. I should have known." She didn't sound as if she approved of tough guys. "Sit down and stay while I fetch the iodine."

A more dashing man would have the right thing to say, meant to charm and make the lass toss him a beautiful smile. A smarter man wouldn't tempt fate and would sit quiet and stoic, determined to do the right thing and not stir up feelings he had no right to. But sadly, he was neither dashing nor smart because he eased stiffly onto the pile of bagged oats stacked against the wall and savored the sight of her. His eyes drank her in, memorizing the slight bounce to her walk, the life that rose up within her here, in the safety of the barn. Gone was the withdrawn and pale girl who'd sat across the table from him. His fingers itched for his pen to try to capture the fairy-tale woman and the adoring cat weaving at her ankles.

What harm can come of this, boy? Nana's voice replayed in his memory. *Time to face your duty. You marry the girl, and you have property. Think of it. Our champion horses would be grazing on McPherson land again. Our name will have the respect it once had.*

But at what cost? He still reeled from his grandmother's betrayal. She was the only family he had left, and he loved her. But if she were here, she would have sold her wedding ring for the money to seal this deal, holding on too tightly to what was past.

"Are you all right?" Fiona waltzed back into the lantern's reach. The light seemed to cling to her, bronzing her as if with grace and illuminating the gentle compassion on her sweet face.

"I've been better."

"Me, too." Every movement she made whispered through the darkness. She knelt before him and set a small box down on the floor, the straw crinkling around her. "Why did you do this? Why did you come?"

"Because my grandmother is dying and I could not say no to her." He fell silent as she gathered his injured hand in her soft, slender ones. Tender emotions tugged within him. "She wants to find what is lost, and I—" He could not finish, the wish and the words too personal.

"I overheard you. You're penniless."

"Aye, and that's not good when you have a sick grandmother needing care." He winced as she untied his bandage and the wound began to bleed fresh. "I regret coming. I've made things worse for you."

"No, you were not the cause." Dark curls tumbled forward like a lustrous curtain, hiding her face. "I will be all right."

"I fear you won't. You cannot look at your parents the same way after tonight."

"True." She searched through the dim interior of the small box at her knee, focusing too hard on the task. She had such small, slender hands. Too tender for what lay ahead of her.

He could sense the hardship she tried to hide because it was too painful to speak of. He knew that feeling well. There was more hardship to come for her and her family, and he didn't like being the one to bear the news. "Before your father told me to get out of his house, he admitted something. The bank is ready to take back the property. At month's end, you all will be homeless."

"So that's why." She shook her head, scattering dark curls and diamond flecks of melting snow. Stark misery shadowed her innocent blue eyes. "Most of the harvest fell in the fields without Johnny to harvest it. Ever since then, we have been scraping by."

"Your father let the harvest rot?"

"He says he is not a working man. He lives as if he still has his family's wealth, although he has not had it since he was probably our age." She uncapped a bottle and wet the edges of a cloth. "Now he needs money to stop an eviction. I see. He ought to know he isn't going to find any takers that way. Who would buy a woman? Especially me."

He bit his lip, holding back his opinion. He was not an experienced man by any means, but Father's lack of decency had given him more than a glimpse of the bad in the world. The land was ideal but mortgaged beyond its value. A man could work himself into the ground trying to keep up with the payments.

How did he tell her it wasn't the land that would attract a certain kind of man?

Unaware of the danger, she leaned closer. Her face was flawless ivory and he could not look away. He did not feel the sting of the iodine. There was only her, this beauty with her gleaming midnight curls and soft pink mouth pursed in concentration. Her touch was the gentlest he had ever known, like liquid gold against his skin. When she drew away, he felt hollowed out, as if darkness had fallen from within.

"I don't know how to thank you for your act of mercy." She cast him a sidelong look through jet-black, lush lashes as she rummaged in the small box once again.

"Just doing the right thing." He remembered how small she had looked in the lean-to, and the horror filling him when he realized she was about to be hit and hit hard.

"And do you often do the right thing, Ian McPherson?" A needle flashed in the lantern light.

"It can wear a man to the bone trying. If only life were more cooperative." He cast her a grin, choosing to keep his stories private. What would she think of him if she knew how he had failed his loved ones? How he had lost his future trying to hold on to the past? He cleared his throat, struggling to let go of things that could not be changed. "I see you were serious about the stitches."

"Is that a note of fear I hear in your voice?"

"Not me. I'm not afraid of a needle and a bit of thread."

"Yes, how could I forget you are a tough one? Grit your teeth, then, for this will do more than sting."

"These will not be my first stitches."

"No, I suppose not." The corners of her mouth drew down as she threaded the needle, and he could easily follow her gaze to where he'd left his cane leaning within easy reach.

Thank the Lord, it was a question she did not ask and so he did not have to answer.

Chapter Five

Homeless by month's end? Fiona's hands trembled as she tied the last knot. The needle flashed in the lamplight as she worked it loose and used her sewing scissors to snip the thread. One last douse of iodine to Ian's wound, and she wrapped it well with clean bandages from the roll she kept on hand in the barn. She could not bear to think of the times her kit had come in handy, for Johnny had been always getting a cut here or a gash there. She could almost hear his voice echoing in the pitch-black corners of the barn, as if whispering beneath the beat of the wind.

No wonder Da wanted her married. It all made sense now. She rose on weak knees, clutching the box. Ian cut quite an impression, even in lantern light. The single flame did little more than chase away a bit of the dark, but it accented his fine profile and the powerful line of his shoulders. What had he given up to come here? A trip from Kentucky was expensive, and if he was all but penniless then this trip had been a risk, too.

"What kind of work have you been doing?" She fit the lid on the box and stood with a rustle of straw.

"Barn work, mostly. Horse work, where I can find it." He glanced briefly at the cane leaning near to him, and the flame chose that moment to flicker and dance, casting him in brief shadow and stealing any hint of emotion that passed across his granite face.

Sympathy welled up within her. That had to be difficult work with a lame leg—or was it simply injured? She stowed the box on the corner shelf, unable to forget how he'd ridden to the rescue. The poetry of him on horseback with the snow falling all around him like grace clung to her, as did the memory of her cheek against his solid back as they rode together through the storm.

"Truth be told, I'm grateful for any work I can get." The shadows seemed to swallow him.

"Me, too." She bit her lip, but it was too

late. The words were already out, her secret already spoken.

"Where do you keep the kerosene?" He moved through the darkness, his uneven gait commanding.

It took her a moment to realize the lantern had sputtered out. "Here, on the shelf, but there isn't much left in the can."

"It will be enough." He stood beside her, close enough to touch. "You work for wages in town, too?"

"I shouldn't have said that. I didn't mean to." She shivered, not only from the chill air driving through the unceiled board walls. "Ian, you won't say anything to them."

"To your parents? No, I will not."

"Good. It will be our secret." She glanced upward into the dark rafters and thought of her savings buried there. An uncontrollable urge to go check on it rolled through her, and she fisted her hands. She could not do so now, not with Ian here.

"What sort of work do you do? Wait, let me guess." His voice smiled, making her wish she could see the shape that grin took on his face. His boots padded across the barn. "You sew."

"How did you know?"

"The extra sewing basket in the empty stall." His footsteps silenced and the lantern well squeaked as it was opened. "I noticed it when I was putting up the horses. You come out here after supper and sew when you can."

"Some afternoons and most evenings." She wrapped her arms around her middle like a shield. "I realized that without my brother, I was as good as on my own. If I wanted something better than my life here, I had to work for it."

A match flared to life like a spark of hope. Although darkness surrounded him, the light bathed him in an orange-gold glow as he closed the glass chimney and carefully put out the match. The single flame struggled to live and then grew, brightening like a blessing on the cold winter's night, a blessing that touched her deep inside. Even standing in the shadows, she did not feel alone.

"Now that our agreement is broken, you are free to marry someone else." He came toward her empty-handed, except for his cane on which he leaned heavily. There was no disguising the tight white lines digging into his forehead.

Was he in pain? The new, gentle light within her remained, growing stronger with every step he took. She didn't know what was happening or why she felt as if the vast barn were shrinking and the high rafters coming down to close her in. Everything felt small— she felt small—as Ian opened the stall gate next to her.

Realizing he was waiting for her answer, she cleared her throat. "I don't want to be any man's wife."

"You don't want to marry?"

"No. I've always dreaded the notion. Our betrothal has been hanging over my head since I was a little girl."

"Were you that frightened of me?" His fingers brushed a stray curl from her face. "I hate to think the thought of me worried you all these years."

"Yes. No." She swallowed; her throat had gone unusually thick. Her thoughts scrambled, too, and she couldn't figure out what she wanted to say. The caress of his thumb against her temple could soothe away a bushel of her fears, and the way he towered over her made her feel safe, as if nothing could hurt her. "I don't want my mother's life."

"Aye, I can understand that." He pushed the strand of hair behind her ear. "What about children? Don't you want a family?"

"I want a real family more than anything." The truth lifted through her, a force she could not stop around Ian McPherson. "When I was a little girl, I would pray every night as hard as I could for God to use His love to heal my family. To make my mother smile and to want to hug me, and to make my father kind. But, as you can see, it did not work. Apparently God's love cannot fix everything that is broken here on earth."

"And that makes you afraid to believe."

"If God's love is not strong enough to heal what's wrong, how could a mere man's be?"

"That's a puzzle I can't answer." He withdrew his hand, but the connection remained. "There is a lot wrong in this earthly life and more challenges than a man feels he can face. But I believe God will make it right in the end. Maybe you will find your family one day, Fiona."

A family? She squeezed her eyes shut, fighting to keep a picture from forming, an image of dreams she once held dear. Loved ones who loved her in return, little children to cherish and raise. Her friends all had hopes for their futures, dreams of a husband and marriage they sewed into their pillowslips and embroidered on their tablecloths to tuck away into their hope chests. But she had no hope chest to fill.

"I don't know if I have enough belief for that. I'll keep faith that you find what you're looking for, Ian McPherson." She did not know what pulled within her like a tether rope tied tight, only that she did not have to think on it. Tomorrow, God willing, the storm would be over and McPherson gone and she would have a new set of problems to face.

She gripped the edge of the door tightly so the wind wouldn't tear it from her grasp. She then slipped out into the bitter night before Ian could move fast enough to help her. Her last sight of him was striding down the aisle with the lantern light at his back. If his kindness had followed her out into the stinging cold, she pretended she didn't feel it.

He had *not* affected her, not in the slightest. Truly. She clung firm to that belief as she battled the leveling winds and sandpaper snow. The blizzard erased all signs of the barn behind her, making it easier to pretend to forget him. She would not let her heart soften toward him. Not even one tiny bit.

But hours later, tucked in her attic room working on her tatting by candlelight to save on the kerosene supply, her mind did return to him and her heart warmed sweetly. Yes, it was a mighty good thing he would be gone tomorrow. She bent over her work, twisting and turning the fine white thread as if to weave dreams into the lace.

Ian stripped the last of the milk from the cow's udder and patted her flank. "There's a girl. All done now."

The mournful creature chewed her cud, narrowing her liquid eyes reproachfully.

"Aye, I'm not Fiona and sorry I am for it." He wagered the animal was sweet on the woman. Who wouldn't be? He straightened from the three-legged stool, lifted it and the bucket with care and climbed over the low stall rails. The black cat let out a scolding meow the instant Ian's boot touched the ground.

"I have not forgotten you, mister." His leg gave a hitch, sending pain streaking up and down his thigh bone. He set his teeth on edge, concentrating on slinging the stool into place on the wall hook and missing the cat underfoot. "You're acting as if you've not seen food for a week. I know you snacked on my beef jerky last night. I caught you in my rucksack."

The cat denied all knowledge of such an

event, crying convincingly with both eyes glued on the milk pail. He crunched through fine airy inches of snow and followed the feline to a bowl on the floor. He bent to fill it and received a rub of the cat's cheek to his chin.

"You're welcome." He left the tomcat lapping milk and wondered how he could get the full bucket through the high winds to the shanty without spilling. Snow drove through the boards and sifted between the cracks in the walls. He'd never seen snow do that before. And the cold. His teeth chattered as he set the pail down to bundle up. How did delicate Fiona do all this barn work in harsh winter conditions, and without help from her father?

Anger gripped him, strong enough that he didn't notice the bitter air when he hauled open the barn door.

"Oh!" A white-flecked figure jumped back. Fiona, mantled in snow and sugar-sweet. "You startled me."

"I seem to be making a habit of it." He ignored the meow of protest from the cat at the sweep of below-zero air into the barn. All he saw was Fiona. Her face had followed him into sleep, haunting his dreams through the night. The hours he had spent in the low lantern light with his notebook and charcoal had not made him grow tired of her dear face. She was only more lovely to him this morning with her cheeks pink and her jewel-blue eyes sparkling.

"Come in." He held the door for her, drawing her into the relative warmth with a hand to her wrist. She felt delicate this morning, as if last night's shock had taken a piece of her.

She brushed past him into the aisle, little more than a slip of a shadow, leaving the scent of snowflakes and roses in her wake. Why such a strong reaction to her? he wondered. Why was being near to her like a bind to his heart? His chest warmed with strange new emotions, and he did his best to ignore them as he let the door blow closed. He was a man with problems, not one in a position to care about a woman or to act on what had troubled him the night through. Best to stick to the plan. He squared his shoulders and faced her. "I was hoping to spare you a trip out into the cold this morning, but I'm too late."

"The milk." She glanced at the two buckets by the door and down the long aisle. She tugged her icy muffler from her face, revealing her perfect rosebud mouth and chiseled chin. "And you've tended the livestock."

"The animals have been fed, watered and their stalls cleaned." He was glad he could do that for her and make her burden lighter, even for this one morning.

"You did my chores." Delight and surprise transformed her. Her flawless blue eyes were compelling as any lyric, her vulnerability captivating as any poem. She waltzed to the nearest stall, her small gloved hands brushing Flannigan's nose. "And done well, too. Oh, Ian, thank you. This is wonderful."

"It's nothing I haven't done every morning at home. Or used to." Sketching her for hours last night had not been enough. He planted his feet, longing to capture the snow glinting like jewels in her midnight-black hair and her shining happiness. "When our stables were full, the morning chores took me from before dawn to noon."

"My grandmother spoke of your family's horses." She swept off her snow-dappled hood. Ice tinkled to the ground at her feet. "I met her when I was a little girl, hardly knee high. She took me on her lap and told me about the thoroughbreds."

"There was never a more lovely sight than a

pasture full of them grazing in the sun, their coats glistening like polished ivory, gold, ebony and cherry wood."

"We have never owned animals like that. Just workhorses. My friend Meredith's family has a very fine driving team, some of the nicest in town, and a few of the wealthier families have horses like that. It's like poetry watching them cross the street."

"Aye, and to see my grandfather's horses run, why, that was pure joy." He ignored the bite of emptiness in his chest, longing for what was forever lost. Failure twisted deep within him, and he couldn't speak of it anymore. "So as you can see, tending two horses and a cow was no trouble at all."

"It hurts you to talk of what is past."

"Aye. Just as it is painful for you to talk about what is to come." He wished he were a different man, one who knew the right thing to do. Leaving could not be right, but staying could be no solution. Fiona wasn't his concern, although he'd spent his life hearing of the pretty flower of a girl he was expected to marry. Perhaps that was bond enough. He cleared his throat. "It was hard when we lost the last of our land. We sold off parcels one at a time, but we could not stave off losing all of it. The hardest part was letting go of the good memories that happened in the house where I was raised. Where my ma would bake cookies for me before she passed away and my grandmother would play the piano in the afternoons. When I was working with my grandfather in the corrals, the music would drift over to us on the wind."

"You are a rich man, Ian McPherson, although I do not think you know it. To have had a family who loved you and memories to hold close like that has to be the greatest wealth there is."

"I've never thought of it that way before." Material wealth had always been a great source of pride in his family, and the loss of it was a great humiliation that had taken the fight out of Grandfather and weakened Nana's heart. He had been fighting so hard to restore his family's wealth, he had not taken the time to consider anything more. But seeing what Fiona had here and how loveless her life was, he saw his childhood with a new perspective. His nana's kindness, his safe and secure upbringing in spite of his father's excesses and tempers and a long apprenticeship with his grandfather, who had taught him more than a profession but a way to face life, as well.

What would you do, Grandfather? He asked, knowing there was no way to be heard, that heaven was not that close. But he thought of the man who had taught him the difference between right and wrong and who had understood his failures, in the end. Failures he felt as powerfully as the bite of pain in his bad leg. He had spent a good part of the night drawing her face and trying to capture her spirit on the page, and those hours stuck with him. When he ought to leave, his feet did not move and a farewell remained unspoken, lodged somewhere near to his heart.

"How is your hand after all that work?"

Not a single word rose up to rescue him as she breezed closer through the gray shadows. With no lantern to light her way, she came like dawn after the night. Sweetly she gathered his hand in hers. Lord help him, because he could not move. As if paralyzed, he stood helpless, captive to her featherlight touch and compassion.

"It doesn't look as if you broke it open." She bent close, scattering dark curls and diamond flecks of melting snow. "Let me change the bandage."

He shook his head, his only protest, and struggled to clear his throat. She affected him, there was no doubt about that, when he didn't want to be. He knew her by memory, those big, wide-set eyes framed by lush black lashes, the slope of her nose speckled with a light scattering of freckles, the curve of her cheek, the shine of her smile and her gentleness that touched him now as she prodded at his wound. A line of concern creased her porcelain brow.

"It will only take a minute and then you can be on your way back home. Come, sit on the grain bags and I'll get started."

The thought of sitting close to her, breathing in her rose-and-snow scent and fighting emotions he didn't want to feel choked him. Panic sped up his uneven pulse. "No need to go to the trouble."

"What makes you think it would be any trouble?"

Aye, there would be trouble if he gave in to the need to stay near her. Trouble in the form he hadn't reckoned on.

A shy man, he said no more, even when she continued to inspect his hand. He stayed the urge to brush the stray untamed curls before they tumbled in her eyes. He fought to wrestle down soft emotions coming to life within him, feelings he did not want to name or examine too closely. "You have taken care of me well enough, Fiona."

"It looks good, so I'll let you have your way, tough guy." She gently relinquished control of his hand. "I should fetch some breakfast for you before you go. Town is a long walk on an empty stomach."

"Is this what you always do? Take care of everyone else? Do you have no one to care about you at all?"

"There's no other family. No one else left alive but my parents." She shook her head, scattering gossamer curls that fell back in place around her perfect heart-shaped face. What a picture she made with her simple gingham dress peeking out beneath her long gray coat and her silken black locks. "Are you starting to worry about me, Mr. McPherson?"

"We are back to being formal, are we?"

"We *are* strangers."

"And yet I've heard of you all my life, lass. I did not think you would be so beautiful."

"Beautiful? No wonder you've never married. You have terrible eyesight and poor judgment."

"Aye, I have been accused of the latter more times than I'd care to admit." He chuckled, a warm coziness coming to life within him. "You enjoy insulting me?"

"What other course do I have?" Her chin went up. "Da might decide to lower his price and then where would I be? It's best to make sure you can't stand the likes of me."

"Wise thinking." He hefted his rucksack from the shadows and settled the strap on his shoulder. "Times might get harder for you, Fiona. You can come to me if you need help, if you need a friend."

"Perhaps I should offer you the same. You might have need of a friend, too."

"That I do." They were too alike, Ian realized, as he buttoned his coat. With family burdens and financial hardships and no clear way to turn, and he wished there was more he could offer her. He grabbed his hat from a nail in the wall and settled it onto his head. His feet did not want to move, although the rest of him was ready. He had not bargained on caring about the girl. He cleared his throat. "I left something for you on your sewing basket."

"A gift?"

"Aye. It was your grandmother's." He hesitated with his hand on the door. "A promise was made long ago that it would be given to you on our engagement day. I think we can agree that you should have it anyway."

"May God go with you, Ian McPherson."

"And with you." He shouldered open the door and the fierce snow pounded against him, cloaking him with white. "Goodbye, Fiona."

"Take care of that hand." She wrapped her arms around her waist, watching as he braced his cane and ambled into the storm. The thick veil of white stole him from her sight long before the door slammed shut, leaving her in darkness.

That was one burden off her shoulders. Ian McPherson, the man chosen for her long ago, had come and gone and her family duty was over. She ought to feel jubilant, or at the very least relieved. She was neither as she knelt to rub the top of Mally's head and dodge him underfoot. She stopped to pat Flannigan and Riley and the emptiness dogged her, a vague feeling that something would never be the same.

Her sewing basket sat tucked in the darkest shadows of the stall, in the soft hay that Ian had freshly stirred and beside the quilts and blankets he had neatly folded. She couldn't make out the two items sitting on the woven basket lid until she knelt close and Mally knocked the edge of a paper with his cheek. The paper flew into the hay like a giant maple leaf, and something sparkled as it fell, too. A small gold locket gleamed dully, the heart shape intricately etched with rosebuds and petals.

The instant her fingers closed around it, she heard Ian's words. *It was your grandmother's. A promise was made long ago that it would be given to you.* The richness, the meter, the lilting kindness of his words rolled through her, one sweet wave at a time, and reminded her of his caring. Of how he had swept a lock of hair behind her ear, how he had stepped out of the darkness to save her from being punished, how his concern for her was as true as an old friend.

She closed her hand around the delicate piece of jewelry and felt the cold metal warm against her palm. Why did the man affect her so much? Why did she remember the richness of his timbre and the character in his voice? She hardly knew him. She would never see him again. He was nothing to her, not really. He was only a story her parents told, a man she had always dreaded meeting, and yet it was as if he had taken something of her she could not replace, something she would always miss. It made no sense, not at all.

What else had he left her? A note? She slid the locket in her pocket and leaned across Mally, who bumped up into her hand. The paper rattled as she drew it out of the straw. Not a note, she realized, squinting at the dark slash of lines and fragile curves. She turned the page around and her pulse skidded to a full stop. Everything within her stilled and she feared it would never start up again. She stared at the exquisite drawing. Airy delicate snowflakes swirled across the snowy white paper, crowning a defiant runaway and a girl with her hand reaching toward the horse. She recognized her own full black curls and the gingham ruffle showing beneath her coat.

His initials were in the right-hand corner, etched next to a snowbound fence post. *Captivated,* he had written below like a title. She closed her eyes, but the image remained as if burned on the back of her lids. *Captivated?* She had almost felt that way with him, when she had held his hand and tended his wound, when he had kept secrets and shadows had darkened his eyes, and when he told her she could turn to him for help. And why did the emptiness he left behind seem so vast?

Mally's meow broke through her thoughts. She opened her eyes to see the cat glaring up at her and yowling again in reprimand.

"Yes, I'm right here and so why am I not petting you?" Fiona ran her fingertips through the cat's long, thick fur. "You are perfectly right. I should never ignore such a good friend."

The feline purred rustily, rubbing her skirts with his cheek. She spent a few moments with Mally before tucking the picture carefully in her sewing basket, and tucking her sewing piecework into her book bag. The locket jingled in her pocket as she went to fetch the milk bucket by the door. It was gone. He must have taken it with him when he left the barn, but she hadn't even noticed. No, she had been far too busy noticing the man.

More proof it was a good thing he was gone. If there was one man who could ruin her plans for the future, it would be Ian McPherson.

Since the work was done, she had no reason to linger in the barn. Her ma needed help with breakfast. She squared her shoulders, drew her muffler around her neck and faced the dying storm.

Chapter Six

"'Mornin', Fiona." Lorenzo Davis saun-tered down the aisle, his boots ringing on the wooden schoolhouse floor. "You're here bright and early today."

Great. Why was he coming in her direc-tion? If she didn't acknowledge him, would he change direction and decide to go somewhere else? Why didn't he try to charm another girl? She poked her needle through the fabric, the click of the needle point against her thimble holding more of her attention than poor Lo-renzo ever would. When the toes of his boots came into sight beside her desk, she could no longer ignore him. "Good morning, Lorenzo."

"What are you working on?"

She peered up at him through her lashes. Surely he wasn't interested in hearing about sewing. She pulled her thread through and considered what to say to him that would be polite but not encouraging, and yet not too friendly to give him any kind of hope. Judging by the clean-combed look of him and that hopeful glint in his polite eyes, he wasn't simply being courteous. She had noticed Lorenzo's interest for a while now.

"A dress," she said simply, and turned her attention back to her next stitch.

"Oh. Uh, you wouldn't be going to join the caroling group at the church, would you?" Nerves hopped in his voice, making it rough and squeaky.

"No, I'm sorry."

"Oh. Okay. Well, you have a nice morning." He took a step back, a wide-shouldered, strapping young man with hurt feelings.

Not what she wanted to do, but she had to be honest. "You, too, Lorenzo."

He nodded once, apparently choosing not to answer, and walked with great dignity back up the aisle. She felt terrible.

"I can't believe you said no." Someone dropped onto the bench seat beside her, occupying the vacant side of the double desk. Lila dropped her calico book bag on the desktop. "Lorenzo is the cutest boy in school."

"Cutest?" She hadn't noticed that, although he was rather good-looking, she had to admit, as she watched him join the popular crowd, headed by their nemesis, Narcissa Bell, near the potbelly stove in the front of the classroom. But his clean-cut good looks could not compare to a certain man's rugged handsomeness and dependable presence, a man she could not get out of her mind. She slipped her needle into the seam to secure it. "Lorenzo is all right."

"He's a complete dream. There isn't one girl in this school who isn't sweet on him, and you turn him down. I heard him. He was going to ask you to join the caroling group with him." Lila, keeping her voice low, opened her bag and pulled out a comb. She began to fluff at her sleek cinnamon-brown hair. "I would have said yes before he could have finished asking me."

"I wish he would have asked you." A terribly tight pressure grew behind her sternum, and it wasn't her corset constricting her breathing. It was Ian. Why did the emptiness inside remain every time she thought of him? It was a mystery for sure.

She folded up her sewing. She had checked on the animals after he'd left her, and they were happy and fed and well cared for. Their stalls spotless, their water bin scrubbed and filled with fresh water. Even the barn cat had been grinning ear to ear while he washed the milk from his whiskers.

Yes, it was a good thing Ian had gone. She pulled off her thimble. "I don't want a beau."

"I know, I know." Lila rolled her eyes lovingly as always. She believed that love happened to everyone when you least expected it, like smallpox attacking when you were vulnerable. Poor Lila. Then again, everyone knew her mother and father had been blissfully happy for a time. She came from an entirely different view of things. "But I would have said yes. Lorenzo is just too too. What are you sewing on? Another piece for Miss Sims?"

"Yes. I almost have the collar set. If I can work the entire lunch hour, I can finish up and get this to her after school." It would be another dollar for her money sock; she might need it sooner than she'd once thought. If her parents were going to lose the farm, then what would happen to them? Where would they go? And what if they found a man they wanted her to marry instead?

I'll run, she decided, thumbing her thimble. The silver gadget winked in the lamplight like an affirmation. It was the only thing she could do. To run away from her best friends and this schoolhouse where she had always been happiest. Snow still fell beyond the windows, reminding her it was a cold world. Making it on her own too soon and with too small of a savings would not be easy. But it would be better than marrying a stranger, than living a life without freedom.

"What? You're going to work through the entire hour again? You've got to eat." Lila's voice drew her back to the classroom. Worry furrowed her oval face. "You're going to ruin your health."

"I've got to get as much work done as I can."

"You work too hard, Fee."

"I don't know what choice I have." Her best choice was still to strike out on her own. So why, then, was she wondering about Ian? With all the snow, would the train arrive on time or not at all? Would he be forced to stay in town awhile longer?

"All right, you have to tell me what's going on." Lila slid her comb into her bag and set it on the floor. "You look like you barely slept a wink last night."

"Sorry. I have a lot on my mind."

"Yes, and why aren't you sharing it?"

How did she tell part of the story without telling all of it? If she spoke of Ian, would it make this strange yawning behind her sternum worse? If she told of why he had left, then would she have to confess what her father was trying to do?

"Just tell me, Fee. Maybe I can help."

"I wish you could." A true friend. Her heart squeezed with thankfulness. Whatever hardships that came into her life, she was grateful to the Lord for softening those blows with caring friends. "Remember Ian McPherson? He came to meet me yesterday."

"What?" Lila's jaw dropped. "You mean that Tennessee guy?"

"He's from Louisville." Mentioning him had been the wrong decision. The emptiness that he had left intensified, like a wound festering. She bowed her head, staring at the folds of delicate green fabric on her lap, but what she saw was the picture Ian had drawn for her. *Captivated,* he'd written. The expert strokes, the skilled rendering of a girl who was too lovely and lyrical to be plain old Fiona O'Rourke. But how she wanted it to be.

"So, what happened? Do you really have

to marry him?" A familiar voice spoke out from behind her. Kate dropped her armload of schoolbooks onto the desk.

"Your parents can't make you, can they?" Scarlet demanded as she took the seat across the aisle.

"No, they can't force me to. Guilt me into it, pressure me into it, scare me into it, yes. But that's not going to happen." Fiona slipped the folded fabric into her book bag with care. "Ian is catching the morning train."

"He's leaving? Without marrying you?"

"Lucky me." Why didn't it feel that way? She didn't want to get married—that had not changed. But something within her had—the belief that there could never be a man she could trust even a little bit.

"Whew. Thank God." Lila's hand flew to her throat. "It might sound romantic in my dime novels, but really having to marry a stranger is downright frightening."

"I'd be scared," Kate put in. "Well, not scared exactly. More like wary. You would want to know that he is a good, honorable man who would never hurt you."

Yes, that was what she was afraid of. Fiona tied the ribbons on her bag, holding her feelings still. Images tried to fill her mind, images of him, noble and fine, but she stopped them. "I was surprised that Ian seemed to be a nice guy."

"That was unexpected." Lila leaned closer. "So, tell us more. Was he good-looking?"

Fiona's face heated.

"He was!" Kate clasped her hands together. "So, did you like him?"

"Why did he come in the first place if he was just going to leave?" Lila asked.

Fiona held up her hands. "Wait. He's gone, so we don't have to talk about it, do we?"

"Yes," her friends answered together, looking shocked that she didn't want to share information about the man they had been wondering about forever.

"It's over. He is not a horrible obligation hanging over my head like a noose anymore." Now he was simply a feeling of loss she couldn't explain or make sense of. He had carried the milk pail to the lean-to before he left, because she had found it was waiting for her inside, safely out of the storm's reach when she'd returned to the house. Only his footsteps and the faint track of his cane in the snow were proof he had been there. A fair walk on an empty stomach and a cold one without a thicker winter coat than his.

Why was her stomach coiling up with worry over him?

"What did I miss?" Earlee wove around and plopped into the seat beside Kate. Bits of driven snow still hung to her blond locks and her face was flushed red from her walk to town. "What's not hanging over your head?"

"Ian McPherson." The name simply popped out and why? Because her stomach had been coiled up with worry over him all the morning through. Had he found a warm place in town? How had his injured leg fared? Was he feeling like this, a confused tangle of sadness and relief?

"The arranged marriage is off," Lila announced.

"And you are free." Kate bounced in her seat.

Free? Her midsection cramped up in knots as she remembered her father's threat. How did she begin to explain that she wasn't free? Not by a long shot.

"Oh, Fee, your parents finally changed their minds!" Earlee clapped her hands with excitement. "That's great news. Yay. You don't have to get married now."

"I feel like celebrating," Kate chimed in. "I'm going to make cookies. No, a cake. I'll bring them tomorrow and we'll have a party at lunch. Just the five of us."

"I'll get some candy from my dad's store," Lila added. "We need to mark this occasion. Fiona is free to find her own beau. Look around, Fee, think of the possibilities."

Her face heated, because she was not looking for a schoolyard crush.

"Class." Miss Lambert strolled to the front of the room and rang her handbell. "School will begin now. Please take your seats."

Saved from having to comment on any of the boys in the room, Fiona gave thanks for the perfectly timed interruption, shrugged apologetically to her friends and slipped her sewing beneath the lid of her desk. Beside her, Lila sighed wistfully as handsome Lorenzo lumbered by and took the back seat two aisles over.

Apparently she was the only girl in school not sighing wistfully. Three other sighs rose around her. When she glanced over her shoulder, Kate, Scarlet and Earlee were all starstruck, their attentions fixed on Lorenzo as he sorted through his stack of schoolbooks.

"I still can't believe you turned him down," Lila whispered. "He could be your beau right now."

"I'm not interested in a—" She started to explain, for probably the nine hundredth time.

"In a beau," Lila answered. "I know."

She had never been one of those girls prone to going sweet on a boy and daydreaming about a future with him. Innocent crushes were fine, her best friends were certainly prone to them, but Fiona was immune. She prided herself on her strength of will and control over her heart.

So why were her feelings about Ian tangled up like a knot in a length of thread? It made no sense. There was so much she wanted to know about him, questions she should have asked. Now she would never know about his grandmother or what his hopes for his future were. While the classroom quieted, she pulled her spelling book from her piles of texts and laid it on top of her desk. It was eight o'clock, but she hadn't heard a train's whistle yet this morning. Had she missed it, or did that mean Ian was only blocks away, still waiting?

Miss Lambert called the twelfth-grade spelling class to the front of the room, so there would be no more wondering. Fiona tucked her book in the crook of her arm, smiled at Scarlet and followed her down the aisle. She passed the frosty windows. Snow was still falling with fury. *Watch over Ian, Lord,* she prayed. *Please touch him with Your grace and make his road easier.*

She thought of the man who had offered her a place to go should she need it. Gratitude, stubborn and tender, crept into her eyes, blurring her vision. She followed Scarlet across the front of the classroom toward the teacher's desk, and she still thought of him.

"I'll be sure and send the telegraph right away for you, Mr. McPherson." The man behind the depot's counter gave an efficient nod as he gathered the coins and the note. "Word is the train is slow, but she's comin'. Just not sure when. If you wander through town, keep an ear out for the whistle."

"Thanks." Ian tipped his hat, pocketed his change and grabbed his cane. His leg hadn't taken kindly to the bitter-cold mile's walk, and while he had thawed out hours ago the healed break in his thigh bone was still putting up a protest.

He ought to be itchy to start the long journey home, but his feet were dragging as he cut across the train station's small waiting room. A crowd gathered around a red-hot potbellied stove, but he wasn't in the mood to sit with a dozen strangers and make small talk. He shouldered open the door, bowed his head against the drum of snow and headed across the street.

Was it luck or Providence that the storm was slowing? Either way, he didn't know, but as sure as it was a December day, there was the steeple of a church a few blocks away and beyond that the bell tower of the schoolhouse.

Fiona. Warmth, unbidden and unwanted, curled around him. He could picture her bending studiously over her schoolbooks with her dark curls framing her flawless face and a little furrow of concentration right above the bridge of her nose. She had been haunting him all morning. Did he get on that train when it came? If he did, what might happen to Fiona? Should he stay behind? And if he did so, what would it cost him and his grandmother? Nana was his only family, surely his responsibility was to her.

That had to be the correct thing to do, he reasoned, trudging through the ruts of ice and snow in the street. But it didn't feel right. He wiped snow from his face with his free hand, squinting against the twirling snow. The shadowed steps were hard to spot covered in white, and trickier to climb up once he was there. The school bell chimed one long merry toll to announce the noon hour. Children's shouts and squeals of freedom rose above the street noise and the dying note of the bell.

Don't think of her, man, he ordered. But his rebellious thoughts went straight to her, wondering if she was with friends, talking intently the way girls did over her pail lunch. Hard not to imagine dark ringlets tumbling down to frame her face and her blueberry eyes flashing with laughter. His heart cracked a little as he hiked down the snowy boardwalk. Hard to say exactly why, because she was not his to care about.

It felt as if she was. He paused in front of a boardinghouse's window. The day's menu was written on a blackboard. Roasted chicken and dumplings looked mighty good, and his stomach rumbled as if it thought so, too. But the sharp note of a train's whistle pierced the falling snow, drawing him away from the window. Looked like God had interceded. It was time to head home.

O'Rourke didn't mind a bit that his poker buddy, the town's sheriff, was paying for his whiskey. His funds were lower than they had been in that long hard stretch before he'd married Maeve. The money from her father's farm, which he'd sold as soon as he'd married her, was long gone, and his plans for McPherson's son to take Johnny's place in the family had come to naught.

"I've got a set amount due the bank or I lose my land." He knocked back the tumbler and waited for the first swallow to burn the back of his throat. "I can't take less than six hundred. Sorry, Dobbs."

"You sure you want to go through with this?" The sheriff, old friend that he was, wasn't the judging type. He tipped back his hat, frowning in thought. "I could get you more, but it'll take a bit. I'll telegraph a few buddies of mine."

"I only got till month's end. Eighteen days."

"Well, that changes things."

Just his luck. O'Rourke drained the glass and banged it onto the scarred wooden bar, thirsty for more. Hard to think in all this noise. One of the dancing girls was tickling the ivories of the warped piano in the corner, and the out-of-tune rendition of "Oh! Susanna" was hard to recognize. Folks in the saloon talked above the music. When a fight broke out at one of the poker tables, he banged his tumbler on the bar to get the bar-keep's attention. If Dobbs couldn't help him, then he was going to need much more than another drink.

"I wish you had come to me sooner, Owen." Dobbs rubbed his beard, still mulling things over.

"You can't help me." Should have known. Luck had been against him at every turn. An O'Rourke shouldn't have to be worrying about living out of the back of a wagon in the dark days of winter. Time was the O'Rourke name put fear into folks. When he was a kid in Lochtaw Springs, no one dared look at him crossways. It was a good thing his daddy wasn't alive to see how the family's outlook had changed. "I've got the horses and the girl. That's all I got, unless I want to hire Maeve out to work in someone's kitchen."

"Now, I didn't say I couldn't help you." Dobbs grinned—slyly, O'Rourke didn't miss that—and tossed a few coins on the bar to pay for their drinks. "I know of someone."

"He'll pay for the girl?"

"Sure. As long as you aren't concerned about getting a wedding ring on her finger."

"I want a son-in-law to work the farm for me."

"Sure, I know, but the man I'm thinking of is always looking. He can pay you right away and, as they say, beggars can't be choosers."

That he knew for a fact. His mouth soured thinking of McPherson wasting his time and that old woman making promises her grandson couldn't keep. He hadn't even thought to doubt her claim. The family had always had deep pockets. It wasn't his fault that he'd been fooled, and it wasn't his fault that Johnny had died to leave him in this predicament. He would send another telegram to that old woman in Kentucky, and in the meantime it was time to do what was best for himself. That's all a man could do in this world.

"As long as she can help out around our place, I don't much care about a ring." He thought of Maeve, sallow-faced and a burden to him. One woman to support was all he saw fit for. "Time to make that girl of mine useful."

"He'll want to get a good look at the girl before he decides." Reasonable, that's what Dobbs was. "He'll want to make sure she's innocent, as you claim. Got a problem with that?"

"Nope, not as long as I get my money."

"If he's happy with her, you'll get it." Dobbs

reached into his vest pocket for a cigar. "How about I bring him along to our poker game tonight?"

"I'll have Maeve bake up that bean soup you like." He searched through his pockets for the last of his tobacco. Either way, it looked like he wouldn't be having to skimp and save when it came to his little luxuries, not anymore. After tonight, his problems would be at an end for some time to come.

Chapter Seven

While the bell tolled in the tower overhead, signaling the end of the school day, Fiona slipped into her wraps in the crowded foyer. She was all thumbs trying to button up. She had to hurry if she wanted to drop by Miss Sims's dress shop on the way home. She had finished her sewing over lunch, and she wanted to pick up more work for tonight. After what Ian had told her, it would be best to make as much extra money as she could before—

Well, maybe she would function better if she didn't look ahead. She fit the last button through, pulled her scarf around her neck and reached for her hood. She would keep walking her path step by step, trusting that she was going in the right direction. Trusting that she wasn't alone.

"I'm definitely going to caroling practice." Lila shouldered close, ignoring the jostle and tussle of the crowd. "Are you sure you don't want to go?"

Oh, it was simple as pie to read what her friend was thinking. Fiona shook her head. Really. She did not want the opportunity to be any closer to Lorenzo. She tucked her hood in place and tied a quick bow. "I'm too shy to sing in front of people."

"You sing at church."

"Yes, but everyone sings there. Even tone-deaf people." Fiona couldn't help it. She cast a glance down the row of hooks and shelving to where Earlee was gathering up her family's lunch tin.

"Hey, I'm not exactly tone deaf. More like tone—hard of hearing." When Earlee smiled, it was like the sun shining. Everyone around her smiled, too. "You'll be glad to know that the caroling group will not have to suffer through my attempts to sing this year. Ma needs me at home."

Smallpox had been hard on Earlee's family, too. Fiona held the door open as her friends paraded through, reminded that rain fell in everyone's life. She should not dwell overly on her own hardships. The snow struck her face like a punch; the storm was still putting up a fight. She thought of the cold walk home and sighed.

"I won't be there, either." Kate swept down the steps. "It's too long of a drive. We wouldn't get home until well past supper and the evening chores. So you town girls will have to tell us country girls all about singing with Lorenzo tomorrow."

"Shh! There he is." Lila gripped the closest girls to her by the arms. Both Kate and Scarlet winced, turning pink as Lorenzo lumbered past.

"Fiona." The strapping young man gave her a brief nod as he headed in the direction of the church. He was persistent, she had to acknowledge that.

The second he was out of earshot, Lila, Kate and Scarlet squealed. "That's it. He likes you."

"Definitely."

"I would die if I were you. He is so nice."

What was she going to say to that? She wasn't interested in a schoolyard crush. And if she pointed out that Lorenzo wasn't nearly as handsome as another man she could think of, then she would have to explain all over again about Ian. Surely her friends knew her well enough to guess at what she might—just might and only a very tiny itty bitty bit—be feeling for her former betrothed.

"Hurry up, Kate," Mr. Schmidt called out from the road, where he was tucked in the family's small, homemade sleigh.

"Coming, Pa!" Kate tossed her braids behind her shoulders. "I'll see you all tomorrow. Lila, don't get into trouble at singing practice. Or if you do, you have to tell us all about it. Fiona, you ought to change your mind about Lorenzo. You're free now!"

Free? That word mocked her. She felt as if chains shackled her to the ground while Kate and her father zipped away behind their fast horse. The falling snow still hid any glimpse of the prairie beyond town, silent and waiting like a reminder. If Da found another groom for her to marry, then she had a plan. She clutched her schoolbag tightly. She would do what she had to.

"Fiona?"

Someone touched her arm. She shook her head to scatter her thoughts, realizing they had taken her away. Earlee was at her side, concern on her heart-shaped face. Her friends watched her with similar worry.

Shame flooded her, scorching her face.

How could she tell them what had happened? That her father was more concerned with having a roof over his head than his daughter's welfare? Lila might not get along with her stepmom, but she was safe and loved. Earlee might not have much, not with nine children in her family, but her father would give his life to keep her safe. Scarlet's family might be unhappy, too, but they would never dream of harming her. As for Kate, her father drove her five miles and back every day so his daughter could have an education. Her caring friends would all support her, but if she told them, then it would bring her sadness into their circle of friendship.

"Fiona?" Earlee touched her sleeve again. "That man there, the one with the black horse and the sleigh, I think he is looking at you."

A man? What man? Panic skittered through her. She swirled toward the road, her mind turning. Ian had gone on the noon train— then again, maybe he hadn't. She had thought of him when she'd heard the train's departing whistle. Had he stayed? Gladness swept through her, as cheery as a Christmas candle. She longed to see his grin and the spark of his poetic blue eyes, but the figure in brown leather standing beside a fancy red sleigh was not Ian.

He hadn't come for her. Logically, at the back of her mind, she knew there was no reason for him to have. But her hopes cracked like a heart broken. Foolish, really, to care so much about someone long gone. It was her decision not to care for any man so much. So it had to be the relentless snow making her eyes tear and not emotions. She was quite in control of her feelings. Really.

"Do you know him?" Lila stepped close, as if to protect her from the stranger's assessing stare.

"He's tipping his hat." Scarlet dropped her schoolbooks. "I don't like the way he's looking at you. Does he know your father?"

"I don't think so." She blinked, trying to bring the man into focus. He was rather short and lean, his features hidden beneath the brim of a black hat. Her da's words replayed in her mind. *If McPherson won't take her, there's others who will.*

No, he wouldn't have found someone so soon. Her bones turned to water. She shook so hard, her lunch pail rattled. No, she reasoned. Certainly not so fast, or someone older than her father. Silver locks peeked out from beneath the man's hat as he tipped it one last time, grinned not entirely nicely at the group of them and climbed back into his sleigh. See how he was leaving? He wasn't approaching her, so she was safe.

Then why was she trembling? Her lunch pail continued to rattle. They all watched the man drive away. Although he never looked back, she couldn't get rid of the strange feeling taking her over, as if her blood had turned to ice.

"Fiona, are you all right?" Lila wrapped an arm around her shoulder.

"You've gone completely white." Earlee did the same.

"He's turned the corner. He's gone." Scarlet tromped back through the hip-high drifts. Only then did Fiona realize her friend had taken off toward the stranger, probably to confront him. That was Scarlet, ever fearless. "I didn't like the way he was looking at you."

"How did you know he was looking at just me?" Her words came out scratchy, like she had a sore throat.

"It was pretty clear." Scarlet was flushed, as if she was ready for a fight. "It was scary."

"Maybe he thought she was someone he knew?" Earlee wondered.

"Maybe." Lila didn't look convinced. "Should we all walk Fiona home?"

"No." She spoke loud enough to drown out their resounding yeses. She had a suspicion she knew what the man had been doing. Her lunch pail was still squeaking and rattling as she knelt to pick up Scarlet's books. "You can't miss singing practice. What about Lorenzo? This might be your big chance to get close to him."

"There will be other chances," Lila answered, stubbornly loyal.

"He's not likely to even notice me," Scarlet confessed.

This was why her throat stayed raw. Her friends were the best part of her life. She looked from Lila and her chin set with determination, to Scarlet dusting snow off her schoolbooks with more ferocity than necessary, to Earlee standing protectively at her side. Surely, this was not the last time she would see them.

"You can't risk it." She shook her head, and snow rained down off her hood. "This might be the turning point. The critical moment when Lorenzo notices one of you and falls deeply in love. So you have to go sing."

"But what about you?" Lila asked.

"I'll be fine knowing my friends are right where they are supposed to be." It was hard forcing her boots to move; the first step away from her friends was the hardest. "Have fun, you two."

"Yeah," Earlee called out. "But not too much fun! Hey, Fee, wait up. You're going too fast."

"Am I?" She was. She'd charged through the snow and onto the broken path by the road like a runaway bull. Her skirt hem and the bottom half of her coat were caked white, and she was huffing as if she'd run miles. Goodness, she was more upset than she'd thought. "Sorry. I've got to stop by the dressmaker's shop. That might take some time, so if you want to head home, I'll understand."

"Ma needs me, but I can spare a few minutes. Besides, poking around the dress shop is fun. There are so many pretty things to look at." Earlee sighed wistfully.

Fine, so she sighed, too. What Earlee hadn't said was that there were so many beautiful things in that shop, things they could never hope to afford. "It is nice dreaming a little, isn't it?"

"Being wealthy isn't what's important in life. It's not what makes you rich. I know that.

But it would be something to be able to own one of those dresses."

"It would." It didn't hurt to dream a little, to wonder what if, right? "If you could have any dress, which one would you pick?"

"The white one in the front window display, with the tiny rosebud pattern. What about you?"

"There's a yellow gingham dress hanging on one of the racks. That's the one I would pick." They turned the corner and tapped down the boardwalk. The town passed by in a blur of lamplit windows and merchants out sweeping the snow off their walks. She dodged a boardinghouse worker with a broom, preferring to think about the possibilities of her daydream, of being someone else with a different life, whose greatest worry was choosing between the exquisite dresses in Miss Sims's shop instead of where she would go, where she would sleep, if she would be safe when she left on tomorrow's train.

"Do you think your pa is going to try to find you another husband?" Earlee's question came quietly, with great understanding. "Was that why that man was staring at you?"

"I don't know for certain, but I'm afraid so." She gripped her book bag more tightly, but she was too frozen inside to feel anything.

"I think I've seen him somewhere before. Like maybe around town, but I couldn't say for sure. Now, if he were Lorenzo's age and half as cute, I'm sure I would have noticed." She flashed her contagious smile, obviously wanting to lighten the mood.

Fiona couldn't help grinning, but it felt like a fake one and it died quickly. Miss Cora's shop was down the next street. It would be hard to tell the kindly lady that this was the last piece she could sew for her. It was time to tie off the loose threads of her life in this small railroad town.

"Look. I think that's him." Earlee nodded once at the red sleigh and black horse parked just up Main. "He's going into the bank, so he must be from around here. We just haven't noticed him before."

That didn't explain the icy ball of dread sitting in the middle of her stomach. She had a bad feeling, and she walked faster down the next street. She didn't feel safe until the man's horse and sleigh were out of her sight.

A nicker rang out from the back of the stables the moment Ian set foot in the Newberry livery stables.

"She's one fine horse." The owner met him

with a pitchfork in hand. "She kept lookin' me over like I wasn't good enough to take care of her. But after I gave her some of my best warmed oats, she at least deigned to let me rub her nose."

"She's a character, all right." He'd missed his girl, his best friend. "I raised her from a foal."

"That right? There are few bonds closer, except for the human kind." The burly man nodded with understanding as he led the way down the main aisle. "Had someone stabling a horse ask if you'd be interested in an offer, but I can see you wouldn't. Don't blame you there."

"No, I want to keep her." Grief cut him deep at all the other horse friends he'd been forced to sell. That made it harder to think of letting another go. The mare caught sight of him, tossing her head and scolding him, as if the last thing she approved of was that he had taken an adventure without her. "Sorry, girl. You'll forgive a poor fellow, won't you?"

Duchess gave him a hard look and blew out a breath through her lips. She lowered her head, allowing him to rub her neck and ears. "Looks like you took good care of her. Thanks, Russell."

"My pleasure. I'll go fetch your saddle," he called over his shoulder.

Alone with his favorite girl, he leaned close, resting his forehead against her warm velvet neck. "You feel up to heading back home?"

Duchess didn't complain, although he thought of the deep drifts, much higher now than when they'd first arrived. She'd struggled with them, which was why he'd stabled her in the first place. He hadn't liked leaving her, but the notion of taking her back out in the hazardous cold and difficult snow gave him pause. Did he leave her here one more night and start fresh come morning? He could always curl up in the stall with her for the night. It was something to consider.

"You would have liked Fiona." He stroked the velvety curve of his mare's nose, just the way she liked it. She sighed deep in her throat, a contented sound. Calm filled him like still water, as it always did when he was around the animals he loved. He missed his horses. He missed his way of life and his calling. *That's* what he ought to be thinking about. That's where his concerns should be. But they weren't. He could not get Fiona

O'Rourke out of his mind. She had burrowed beneath his skin and claimed a part of him.

Duchess nickered low and sweet, leaning into his touch as if she were asking to hear more.

"Nana was right about her." If betrayal panged deep within his chest, he paid it no heed. Whatever his grandmother had done, she had done it for him out of love. He could not fault her for that. And if places new and surprising within his heart seemed to open for the first time upon thinking of Fiona's dear face, then he denied that well and good. Aye, a smart man would not acknowledge anything that could not aid his life's plans.

"The farm was not in good shape. The barn poorly maintained, the fence posts sagging in the fields. But the land was something. I like these wide-reaching plains. What do you think, Duchess?"

She tossed her head up and down as if in agreement. He supposed the endless prairie called to her spirit, too, calling her to race the wind. Unbidden, the image of Fiona sprang into his mind, the one that had kept him up much of the night trying and failing to get it down on paper. He had captured the curve of her cheek as her dark curls brushed it, the bold set of her porcelain jaw and the swirl of her skirt when she had first turned in that storm to face him. The first moment he had seen her face was emblazoned in his mind, and he'd been able to replicate her big, honest eyes, perfect sloping nose and rosebud mouth. What he'd not been able to capture was the strength and radiance of her spirit.

Somewhere a bell chimed, muted by snowfall and distance, marking the time. Didn't sound musical like a church bell. A school bell, he figured, announcing the end of the school day. Ten miles down the rails, Fiona would be leaving the warm schoolhouse. Would she be walking with friends? Did she get her sewing done?

His gut twisted tight, a sure sign he was acting against his conscience.

"Sure is a nice saddle you've got." Russell lumbered into sight. "Don't see gear like this in these parts."

"Don't tell me you've got an offer for it, too."

"If you're interested, let me know. No pressure." With a friendly grin, he hefted the saddle onto a nearby sawhorse. "If you're in these parts again, I hope you drop by. I sure would appreciate your business."

"I will." His mind had already decided. He had lost all reason and erased the long list of his obligations back home. Of his grandmother depending on him. What about the debt he was in the middle of settling, the horses needing his care and the weight of his family's fallen dreams? They felt like nothing against the image of one woman he could not forget.

Duchess bumped his shoulder to get his attention.

"It's all right now, girl," he told his mare. "I won't be leaving you again."

In the distance he heard another sound, the approaching blast of the westbound train. The train that would take him back the way he'd come and back to Fiona's door.

What do I do, Lord? He glanced upward, hoping that the Good Father could see him in spite of the storm. There was a choice he had to make—one was sensible, the other borne on emotion alone. Only God would know the consequences of each. Only God could lead him the right way. He bowed his head to pray.

Another dollar. Fiona tied the top of her money sock into a knot. It wasn't a fortune, but the twenty-three dollars in coins would have to be enough. Her stomach knotted tighter as she tucked the thick bundle into the little wooden box her grandmother had gotten her. It was meant to be a jewelry box, but she'd had no jewelry to store in it until now.

She brushed the locket with her forefinger. The memory of her grandmother was dim, but she'd been a smiling, gentle woman who smelled of cinnamon rolls. Maybe it was because she had been baking them that day Fiona's family had come to visit. There had been an argument, and she had never seen the woman or heard from her again.

Let me tell you about the man you will marry one day, her grandmother had said in her quiet way. Like music the words came, although she did not sing them. Fiona remembered being a little girl, snuggling close to her grandmother's side, wanting to hear more of the story. Her grandmother had obliged. *Ian is a mere boy, barely a year older than you, but I hear he already has his grandfather's gift with horses. He's a born horseman. They say McPherson thoroughbreds are the prettiest sight in all of Landover County. You will live there one day, my dear, and gaze upon the green fields where the magnificent horses race in the sunshine. What do you think of that?*

Remembering the love that had shone in her grandmother's words drove the cold from the air. She realized she was smiling as she closed the box's fitted lid. She had forgotten the musical sweetness of the story; over the years the family's agreement to marry the McPherson heir had lost all wonder. Da spoke of his exploits of drinking and gambling and pranks done together as boys until she began to see Ian's father and Ian himself as the worst nightmare she could dream up.

She'd been wrong. Her smile lingered, remembering the kind, strong man. It was tempting to want to turn to him. She *almost* altered her plans to run westward and go to Landover County instead.

Foolish, though, wouldn't it be? She slid the small box beneath the loose floorboard and laid the wooden planks flat to hide her treasures. She knew Ian's offer of help had been a genuine one, but he had troubles of his own. He did not need her to add to them.

The barn door flew open, startling her, and cracked against the wall. The animals cried out in alarm, trampling nervously in their stalls below. Mally flew from his soft bed in the hay beside her with his claws out and tail bristling to dive for cover. Likewise, she covered the floorboards with an old burlap sack and a hunk of hay.

"Fiona!" Da's shout didn't sound as angry as it usually did, echoing in the shadowed rafters. "Get down here. We're having guests to supper."

"Guests?" Her knees weakened as she pushed to her feet. What guests? A man like the one today? Fear gripped her. She still had time to grab a few things and meet the four o'clock train. If she hurried and ran most of the way, she could make it.

"My turn to host the poker game." Da came to the base of the ladder, his gaze pinning her in the half-light. There was warning in his eyes and in the hard set of his jaw. That always spelled trouble for her. "I'll expect you to help your ma."

"It's Thursday," she realized. One of Da's regular poker nights. Her knees turned watery with relief.

"Get your lazy self down here. I brought you up to work, and it is work you'll be doing or else. I don't want any nonsense tonight. You hear me, girl?"

"Yes, Da." She cast one last look toward

her hidden box. The wind gusted against the north wall of the barn, howling as if in protest. She gripped the top rung of the ladder, wishing she could ignore the clench of nerves deep inside.

It's going to be all right, she told herself, but in truth, she could not be sure.

Chapter Eight

The distant *toot, too-oot* of the westbound train called across the prairie, muffled by the lessening snowfall and by the thick, panicked pulse thudding in her ears. Was it four o'clock already? Fiona stopped stock-still in the middle of the yard, forgetting the empty buckets in both hands, forgetting that Ma had a sharp eye on her. She shivered, but not from the cold penetrating her coat. Her parents had kept her busy with one task after another, and every time she slipped away to pack a few necessary clothes, they called her to do some other chore. And now here she was, home and not on the depot's platform with a ticket in hand.

And why was the train on time in this weather, instead of running behind? Oh, why couldn't it have been fifteen minutes late, just today? That was all she needed to get the water from the pump and slip back out of the house.

"Fiona!" Ma's shrill anger rang loud enough for the neighbors, a quarter of a mile away, to hear.

Or at least it seemed that way. Fiona jumped, her heart thudded and the bucket handles slid from her grip.

"What are you doing, standing around like a loon? Get to work." Face ruddy, mouth drawn tight in anger, Ma stood at the top step, her spatula raised as if ready to strike. "An important visitor is to come, and if he sees you lolling about like an idiot, your father will have your hide. You understand?"

A visitor? What visitor? Surely this could not be another would-be husband for her, and so soon. "I thought it was just Da's poker night."

"And he is coming to play cards, too."

All the daylight drained from the sky. Winter's cold burrowed deep within her. "I won't do it, Ma. I'm not going to marry anyone."

"We are your parents, and you will honor us as the Bible says. You will do what you're told." Ma's face sharpened, and a harsh look twisted her features.

What could she say to that? Anything would be seen as disrespectful, and even God's word was clear. A child must honor her parents, but surely He did not mean for her to obey in this. Snowflakes struck her face like tears. In town, a mile away, the train was at the depot, idling on the tracks. Each moment that passed was one moment closer to the train's departure. If she hurried, left her belongings but grabbed her treasure box, she could run to town before the train left. But if her parents spotted her, then Da would come after her on one of the horses. She could not run fast enough to evade him.

"Fiona!" Ma's voice hit like a slap to her cheek.

She knelt to retrieve the fallen buckets, but she missed one of the metal handles and had to reach for it three times. Out of the corner of her eye, she caught her mother turning with an economical swish of her skirts and disappearing inside the lean-to. Time and defeat had stooped her spine, and misery covered her like a shawl.

If she did not run, would that be her one day? She shivered, despair heavy within her.

Snow grabbed at her boots just like dread at her heart. If she married as her parents said it was her duty to do, would life always be this way? Would one day follow another, filled with hard work and a cold man's cruel words? When the color in her hair had faded to gray and her face became roughened with deep lines, would she, too, speak harshly with unhappiness?

She reached the well and fit one bucket's handle into the groove. If she squinted, she could make out the shadowy boxes of the town's buildings. *Run.* The wish rose up as if from her soul, and longing filled her. She wanted to hitch up her skirt and take off through the fields straight to the depot. To her surprise, she was already twisting away from the hand pump, reaching for her skirts when a hard voice stopped her.

"Fiona! Stop fooling around." Da appeared around the corner of the shanty. "Come stable this man's fine animal."

She swirled to a stop, vaguely noticing the bucket had fallen from the pump and hit the snow with a ringing clank. Her gaze went straight to the black horse standing obediently at Da's side and the short, bony man next to it.

The man from the schoolyard. The wind

seemed to push at her, urging her to run. But it was too late.

"Come here, child." A wide hat brim shaded the man's face, but he reached toward her, holding out his hand. The glove he wore looked to be of the finest leather. "Come meet my horse. He's a purebred. There isn't one finer in all of Angel County."

"You had best not trust him to me, then." She did not know exactly why she feared the man. Perhaps it was his small smile that didn't look genuine, or the jovial way Da tried to wave her closer.

"Come on, lass. You're sweet on the critters. Come take care of this gentleman's horse so we can get started with our game." Da nodded to her, as if everything was going to be all right. He wasn't even angry with her for the fallen bucket or the fact that she'd been dawdling when it came to fetching water for his supper.

Warning enough that something was wrong. She could not make her feet move.

"Don't make me come get you." The warning came subtly and with a cold promise. "I'll be makin' sure you regret it if I do."

"Yes, Da." She left the buckets where they lay and tried to uproot her shoes from the earth. Her pulse rattled like dried leaves in a wind and she shuffled forward. She felt afraid, although she couldn't say exactly why.

"Nice to meet you, miss." The stranger tipped his hat to her, as a gentleman might. He looked dapper with his tailored clothes and long duster. But there was something in his cold liquid eyes, something she didn't understand.

"Sir." Her curtsy was shaky under her father's watchful eye. The wind swirled against her as if to grab her away, and the departing train's whistle mocked her with what might have been. She gripped the reins her father held out for her and turned on her heels.

It wasn't a terrible thing—surely this would go as before. The man would stay to supper and then speak with her father. She still had time. Relieved, she clucked to the horse and he followed her obligingly. She was panicking for nothing. It wasn't as if the minister was coming. Wedding preparations took time. She swiped the snow from her eyes with her free hand. If this really was a man wanting to marry her, she could take her money to school with her tomorrow morning and walk to the depot. Her parents would think she was at school. And chances were this man wouldn't be interested in a wife less than half his age. What were her folks thinking? It just went to show how desperate they were.

She wrestled the barn door open and ignored the flickering anxiety in her midsection. She had to stay calm. Rational, instead of acting on fears that weren't real. She led the horse into the aisle. Flannigan neighed out a warning, for this was his barn. Riley reached out as far as his stall would allow, straining against the groaning boards. The cow, chewing her cud, seemed unimpressed with the newcomer. By the time Mally let out a meow from the overhead rafter and reached down to try to bat at her, the knot in her stomach had eased.

See? Everything was fine. Likely as not, this evening would turn out much like Ian's visit. The instant Da mentioned that money would be part of the bargain, the old guy would head out the door so fast he would be nothing more than a blur.

The hinges creaked, and the inside of the barn went dark. It took her a moment to realize someone had shut the door. Flannigan trumpeted in protest. The horse she held tugged at his bits. They were no longer alone.

"Hello?" She dropped the reins and felt her

way to the first main pole. She groped for the match tin, bumping the lantern. It rocked on its nail with a scraping sound, like fingernails on a blackboard.

"I thought we oughta get better acquainted." A stranger's voice lifted out of the shadows. Footsteps padded toward her on the hard-packed earth. His voice sounded closer. "I hear you're lookin' for a man."

"You heard wrong." She found the edges of the match tin and lifted the lid. "My father is looking for money."

"A pretty penny, too, but then you are a very pretty girl." His shadow hulked out of the blackness, within arm's reach.

Tiny fissures of alarm snaked through her. She struck the match, chasing away the darkness. Sure enough, the black-horse guy was within hand-shaking distance. She touched the flame to the lantern's wick. "You aren't really interested in me, are you? It's the farm. Is that why you're here?"

"I'm a lonely fellow, and lookin' to settle down. I got my own place east of here."

"Lonely?" She blew out the match, wishing she could extinguish her bad feeling as easily. "I would make a terrible wife. You ought to find someone else. Maybe someone your age? Maybe you could attend church. There are plenty of nice older ladies there."

"Now I know why your pa is desperate to get rid of you." A sour expression crossed the man's ruddy features. "You've got a smart mouth. That can be cured."

"I doubt it." She closed the lantern's squeaky door. "Why don't you go play cards. I've got work to do, and I—"

"Did I say you could talk?" His temper flared, as if out of nowhere. "I like what I see, but you have some learnin' yet to do."

"Leave me alone, you—" She didn't see the blow coming, it was so fast. His palm shot out and connected to her cheek. Pain bulleted through her skull, and white stars danced in her head. Her knees no longer held her upright. He'd hit her, she realized, as her head cracked against the wood post, and she hit the ground on her back. She tried to focus on the rafters overhead, but they were blurry. Her ears rang like church bells.

"I don't like sass and I don't take orders." He towered over her, fists clenched, ready to swing again. "Listen here, missy. You will do what I say."

Fear crackled through her nerve endings as she inched backward. Her father was in

the house, and she knew the sheriff was, too;
she'd seen him arrive. "I don't understand
why you would want to marry me."

"Who said anything about marrying you?"
He grabbed for her arm and she rolled away.
"My last gal run off, and I have need of some-
one to cook and clean and keep me warm."

Shock choked her. She gasped for air, but
nothing came. Just a garbled sound, a terrified sound. Dimly she wondered what would
happen to her. If he intended to take her with
him tonight, with her father and the sheriff watching to make sure she obeyed. She
would have no chance to say goodbye to her
friends. They would go to school tomorrow
and know nothing of why she wasn't there.
The future she'd wished and saved for, the
one with hopes for a happy life working at
some pleasant job in a nice town and her own
little house one day—all that would vanish.

"Git up!" The stranger grabbed for her
again.

She leaped to her feet, evading him. Flannigan neighed angrily. Riley lunged and reared
in his stall. They sensed the danger, too. What
else did this man intend to do to her? Her fingers closed around the worn smooth wood

of the pitchfork handle. She presented it, tines out.

"Go away." She might bc able to scare him off, or make him angry enough to run and get her da. That would give her the time she needed. Time to run and hide in the falling darkness.

"How dare you give me orders!" His face twisted with rage and he lunged toward the pitchfork as if to rip it from her hand. But he was jerked off his feet from behind.

"Fiona? It's me." Ian McPherson emerged from the shadows, as strong as a hero, as shadowed as twilight. "It's all right now, I promise you that."

"I'm dreaming you up, aren't I?" She started quaking so hard the pitchfork shook. It was a cruel trick her mind was playing on her.

"The last thing I am is anyone's dream, lass." He looked real enough as he hauled the cursing man to the door by the back of his collar, handily, as if he were carrying a varmint by the scruff of the neck. "Reckon it's a good thing I've come back."

"I'll not argue with that." A good thing? A blessing it was. He had come just when she needed him most. She watched in disbelief as he deposited the man outside in the storm, exchanged heated words with him and strode inside to grab the black horse by the reins. When he slammed the door shut, they were alone.

"It did not take long for you to get into a wee bit of trouble." He ambled toward her, his limp pronounced, as if he'd strained his injury. "I was right. Your father wasted no time finding a man to take my place."

"You were the far superior candidate."

"Your nose is bleeding. Sit down." He took a handkerchief from his pocket and shook out the folds. "Tilt your head back. Pinch the bridge of your nose."

"I don't have time." Her head might be foggy and now that Ian mentioned it, blood was running down her face, but she couldn't stand here. The man—with Da—would be back. "Could you saddle Flannigan for me?"

"Saddle him? What for?" He dabbed gently at her nose, close enough that she could see the day's shadow whiskering his chin and smell the winter wind on his coat.

"I don't think I can do it. My legs are like water." She let him tilt her head back, the metallic taste of blood on her tongue. His callused fingertips pressed against the bridge of her nose and pinched it, a gently soothing touch. Why was he doing this?

"You can't go anywhere while you are bleeding hard. I hope you weren't sweet on that fellow."

"Hardly. I was prepared to introduce him to the sharp end of the pitchfork when you came."

"So I saw. I'll have to remember that the next time I think about making you angry." A dimple teased at the corner of his mouth.

Had he always been so very handsome? His perfect blue eyes had lighter blue speckles in them. How on earth had she not noticed that before? Or how comforting the sheer size of him was, that when he stood between her and the rest of the world, she felt safer than she had ever been. She longed to lay her cheek against his chest and rest, to know that nothing would hurt her as long as the moment lasted. She watched him through her lashes, noticing the squint of concern at his brow and his wince as he wiped the last of the blood from her chin. How noble he looked, burnished by lantern light and framed by darkness.

There was something about him that stirred up emotions she didn't understand. Gentle, hopeful feelings that were surely simple schoolgirl silliness. She saw it all the time, girls going sweet on a boy. Look at her best friends; as much as she loved them, it was so easy for them to fall into an innocent crush. But she was not that girl. She did not believe in love. She could not believe in noble men. So why was she leaning toward him? Why did she wish that he could be what she needed?

I don't need any man, she reminded herself. What she needed was to gather her common sense, toss these foolish thoughts right out of her head and make wise use of the time she had to escape. Da would be coming, and then it would be too late.

Please, God, she prayed, *just a little help.*

"The bleeding is slowing." He pressed a clean, folded handkerchief into Fiona's free hand. "In case it starts up again."

"Thank you." Her fingers squeezed his before she let go. "Something bad would have happened to me. I know it."

"You never figured on being glad to see me." He pushed a lock of hair out of her eyes.

"I'm grateful, Ian."

"Grateful is how I'm feeling, too." He could make out the pain on her delicate features. Far too much sadness for one small woman. She broke him, that's what she did, changing him as surely as stars changed the night. "Where are you going?"

"Away from here. My father will be pounding through that door, and I don't intend to be here when he does." She grabbed hold of a rung and started to climb, her skirts swishing and her face ghostly white in the half-light. "Why did you stay, McPherson?"

"Thought I would stick around and do some sightseeing. This is mighty pretty country."

"Did you miss your train?"

"No. I got as far as Newberry, where I stabled my horse."

"Your horse?" Her voice echoed like a stretch of music in an empty church, drawing him closer.

"I rode horseback all the way from Kentucky." He grabbed a rung and followed her into the rafters.

"It's winter outside."

"Aye, I was well aware of that as I slept night after night on the frozen ground." He climbed over a low beam, and the sight of her kneeling in the hay was a sweet sight. Her hair was atumble, bits of dried grass and seed clung to her clothes. She looked like a lost orphan in need of a home and a hot meal. Wanting nothing more than to be her shelter, he knelt beside her. "What? You think I have money to waste on comfortable hotel rooms?"

"Then how come you arrived on the train?" The question crinkled her forehead, completely adorable.

Hard it was to look at her bruised and swollen face and fear staining her perfect blue eyes. He would do anything to take away her fear. He would give up everything so she could be safe. "I got as far as Newberry, but the drifts were too much for Duchess. She's expecting a foal come spring, so I stabled her in town and bought a ticket here. It was only twenty miles, so the journey did not cost much."

"You rode the train out of consideration to your horse?"

"Aye, it was a dollar I did not want to spend, but she is the best friend I have. What is a fellow to do? You, on the other hand, cannot catch a train until tomorrow."

"I'm not going to take the train." She swept hay from the floorboards in front of her. "Why did you come back?"

"It seems I had no choice." He thanked the Lord for leading him back. What would have happened had he not followed his conscience? His stomach knotted. He couldn't stay the urge to caress the side of her soft cheek with his knuckle. A gentle touch, and he wished it could take away her pain, heal what was bruised and battered.

"Did you leave something behind?" She hauled up a small length of board.

"You might say that." There was nothing to say but the truth. "I could not make myself ride another step east, so I followed my heart back to you."

"Back to me? I don't understand." She pulled out a small box, which she hugged to her. The first hint of moonlight streamed over her as if it, too, wanted to hold her dearly.

"I'm here to help you." It was the deepest truth he had ever known on this earth, a commitment that bound him as surely as God was in the heavens. "I'm going to make sure you are never frightened like that again."

Duchess chose that moment to whicker, a low nervous sound in her throat. Flannigan neighed, and a thud of steeled horseshoe connected with a wood wall. Sounded like trouble was coming. Ian was already rising when the barn door slammed open like a hammerstrike.

"Fiona! What in blazes is going on in here?" O'Rourke's color was high from fury and whiskey, made brighter by the lantern he carried. "McPherson. What are you doing here?"

"I've reconsidered the offer." He pushed the wooden box back into the hiding place. "Fiona is my fiancée from this moment on."

He heard Fiona's gasp of shock, and if he feared she would hate him for it, then he ignored that fear. He wanted to give her time to hide what had to be her money, so he climbed over the beam and down the ladder to discuss the rest of his terms with O'Rourke.

Chapter Nine

Fiona is my fiancée from this moment on. Ian's words rang in her head like a funeral bell with every step she took carrying the water buckets back to the house. Da had ordered her out of the barn and the rise of temper ruddy on his face made her knees knock. She'd fled into the frigid twilight, longing to know what the men were discussing.

How could she feel so much gratitude toward Ian and hate him even more? How could Ian do this to her? She'd trusted him. *I followed my heart back to you,* he'd said. Trying to charm her, no doubt, when he really saw her as a means to get the land he couldn't buy any other way.

Wasn't that a man for you? She felt torn apart, like the aftermath of a twister leaving rubble in its path. The edge of the bucket slammed against her shin with a clang and a snap of pain.

Pay attention, Fiona. She shook her head, trying to scatter her thoughts, but it did no good. Her mind looped straight to Ian, how tenderly he had cared for her and his kindness in the loft. Before he'd announced he intended to marry her against her will. What happened to being friends?

"Hurry up, you lazy girl," Ma bellowed from the doorway. "You have caused enough trouble for one evening. That man, the one who came to meet you, he left angry. You have much to make up for, young lady."

Miserable, she stumbled up the steps, spilling water as she went, hardly able to see where she was going. Her vision was still blurry, and her nose was throbbing. She let the kitchen door slam shut and heaved the buckets onto the small counter.

"You are getting snow everywhere." Ma whirled from the stove. She had to notice the blood and the swollen cheekbone, but she simply pointed her spatula at the mess on the floor. "I have enough to do. You clean that up and then you get to work."

"Yes, Ma." She grabbed the broom and

dustpan and knelt to swipe snow chunks into the pan. Her pulse thundered in her ears, drowning out Ian's remembered words. *I've reconsidered the offer.* He had gotten as far as Newberry and what did he do, start thinking about what awaited him in Kentucky? His family lands—gone. His family fortune—spent. What did he care about her future when he was more concerned with his?

"You had best be on your good behavior when your da gets in this house. We are not happy with you, Fiona." Ma turned the ham slices in the fry pan one by one. "We've a house full of your father's friends and Mr. Newton storms into the house saying you've attacked him. We're to lose our home because of you. You're a thoughtless, selfish girl, Fiona, and I can't stand the sight of you."

She leaned the broom in the corner by the door and emptied the snow into the waste bucket. She had done the right thing all her life. She had been quiet when her parents told her to be. She did the work her parents told her to do. She prayed day and night. She studied her Bible, she lived faithfully and she did well in school. And for what?

She washed her hands in the corner basin, breathing in the sharp scent of the plain lye soap. All she could see was her life in this kitchen, working in the half-light of a turned-down wick to save on the cost of kerosene day after endless day. That was her future unless she decided on another course. With twenty-three dollars to her name, how far could she get? She dried her hands on the small towel and hung it neatly on the stand's hook. Ian was the problem. Would he let her go?

"Stop lollygagging." Ma checked on the simmering soup with a slam of a pot lid. "Supper's almost ready."

She grabbed a towel and knelt to rescue the biscuits from the oven. They were golden-topped and fluffy, so she carried the sheet to the table and filled a waiting basket.

As she placed the basket on the table, an uneven gait tapped outside the kitchen door. Ian. Her mind looped to him like a lasso arcing through the air. Seeing him towering over her protectively, hauling the man away, feeling his caring touch to her cheek, hearing the kind rumble of his voice made her feel confused—angry and used and needing his tenderness again. What had he promised her? *I'm going to make sure you are never frightened like that again.* That's what he'd said, probably thinking that by marrying her he would be keeping her safe. That was probably his justification for his broken promises.

The door squeaked open, and there he stood looking like goodness itself. Her hatred peaked. A pressure built inside her throbbing head. If only part of her still didn't care—the stupid, needy part of her that had believed in him. And it hurt worse than any blow.

"Smells good in here, ladies." He stepped into the room as if he belonged there.

"The men are in the front room." Ma glanced at him with what passed for surprise, but after a huff went back to her cooking. That would change once Da told her what Ian had done.

Fiona ignored the silent apology that radiated off him and hefted the ironware from the shelf. The rattle of the stacked dishes betrayed her. She was not calm. She was not unaffected. She wanted to hurl the plates at him; she wanted to turn time back like resetting a clock and stay in that place where she had trusted him, where he was her friend.

Hurt and outrage blazed through her, staining her vision red, making the top of her head feel a strange pressure. She turned her shoulder and passed the plates around the table, holding back two for her and Ma. They would eat in the front room, out of the way of the men. Their loud raucous language and laughter roared through the thin board walls. Da's voice joined then, jovial. Then, why wouldn't he be?

The last plate hit the table with a clink. She kept her gaze down and her back turned. Sure, she could feel the sensation of his gaze traveling over her face, trying to make eye contact, perhaps wanting to exchange a smile or two. Maybe he was even hoping she would forgive him. He had no notion she was breaking inside, losing the little drop of faith she ever could have had in a man.

She yanked open the drawer and counted out forks, knives and spoons. She told herself she didn't care as his step tapped close and he waited for her attention. Turning her back, she didn't acknowledge him. If she felt his hurt feelings like a slap to her cheek, she ignored it. She did not care at all. Absolutely not. Not a little bit.

She sorted through the flatware, aware when his slow step left the room. Shame filled her. She laid a fork and spoon on a plate with a clatter. She was lying and, worse, it was to herself.

* * *

Seeing how Fiona despised him made something within him die a little. All through the meal at the kitchen table, with men he neither knew nor liked, he thought of her in the front room, eating quietly with her mother. There had been nothing quiet about the anger flushing her cheeks and flashing in her eyes. He could still hear the echoing clatter and clinks and clanks as she'd set the table, angry sounds he could not dismiss.

"That woman. Gettin' slow." O'Rourke ambled back to the table like a king settling onto his throne. "Don't know why I keep her some days."

"She's a fine cook, Owen." One of the men patted his belly and leaned back in his chair. "Can't say my Martha can make biscuits like that."

Footsteps padded closer and the rustle of skirts grew louder. Fiona was coming. He felt her nearness like a touch to his spirit. He knew the exact moment she entered the room because the sharp edge of her anger hit like a dagger's blade to his back.

She will understand, he argued with himself, but it did not ease the bad feeling in his gut. He'd hurt her with his actions. O'Rourke had burst into the barn before there was a chance to explain, to try to make things right with her. Now, he feared it was too late. The damage had been done.

"Hurry up!" O'Rourke spat to the women, his features turning narrow and mean as he pulled a deck of cards from his pocket. "We don't got time to waste."

Ian's fists curled, but he stayed in his seat. He was too reactive where Fiona was concerned. Too involved. Too invested. He didn't know how it happened, but it took all his self-discipline to sit still. The need to protect Fiona beat inside him with a blizzard's fury. But judging by the way she kept her back to him as she snatched his plate and bowl from the table, he guessed she didn't want him coming to her aid any time soon. Maybe never.

Looked like he'd made a mess of things, and he was sorry for it. He pushed out of his chair.

"Stay and play, McPherson," O'Rourke commanded.

"I'm not a gambling man." He snagged his coat from the row of wall pegs. He may have been talking to her father, but his gaze stayed fixed on Fiona. Red stained her face, and the muscles in her jaw bunched and jumped. She kept her head down as she worked, taking plate after plate and stacking them into the fold of her arm. Her nose was swollen, her cheek was bruising, her face ashen. Some emotion too elusive to name tangled within him. He shrugged into his coat, wishing he knew how to make things right for her. All he saw was a long string of heartache for them both.

God may have led him here, he realized, but it was not the easiest path. Maybe not even a possible path. He could lose what little he had left of his dreams and his grandmother's hopes for the family.

"We're all gambling men." O'Rourke's tone might have been jovial, but something glittered in his eyes. Something mean and cold. He wasn't happy that the lowlife varmint who'd attacked Fiona had decided he didn't want her after all. Too cantankerous, he'd said. That meant O'Rourke had to settle for what Ian was offering or wait for another offer for his sorry piece of land and his innocent daughter.

Bitter fury filled him, and Ian's mouth soured as if he'd tasted something vile. He did not have time to examine it because Fiona stayed on his mind. The stubborn jut of her delicate chin was the only sign of her fury as she swept to the small corner counter and set the plates down next to the wash basin.

"Every day is a wager," O'Rourke was saying. "You never know if you're going to win, draw or fold."

"A man's lot in life is uncertain." Hard not to agree with that. "But if he works hard, trusts God and does the right thing then most times it turns out."

"I've learned it's better to take matters in your own hands. Sit down, McPherson. I'm bein' hospitable."

"I'm not interested in your brand of hospitality." He tipped his hat, settled it on his head and wrapped his hand around the battered wooden latch. Fiona was within reach, hating him. Everything within him yelled to go to her, to lay a comforting arm around her delicate shoulders and whisper in her ear. Let her know it was okay. The misery pinching her battered face destroyed him.

But he feared O'Rourke's wrath. The man was not happy with the bargain struck; well, he wasn't alone in that. Ian didn't like it, either. Enough responsibility weighed on his shoulders, and now he had another. Fiona, carving shards from the bar soap, each falling into the steaming basin with a plop. Tenderness gathered like a storm within. If he comforted her now, her father would see it and guess how much the girl meant to him.

Worse, he feared Fiona would push him away, so he drew open the door. Regret clawed at him. He'd hurt her every bit as much as the man responsible for the dried blood staining her collar. He hated that. He forced his feet to carry him out of the room feeling less than the man he strived to be.

Alone in the lean-to, the cold and dark wrapped around him like a shroud.

Her parents' voices murmured through the floorboards as she moved in the half dark of her little attic room. Moonlight filtered through the small window enough for her to see. She folded her last pair of woolen long johns into the top of the secondhand satchel her friend Meredith had given her.

However was she going to stand to leave her friends behind and without saying goodbye? She snapped the top closed and wished she could close her feelings as easily. But no luck. Her gaze strayed to the window and across the darkness to the barn, where the faint lick of a candle danced and flickered between the cracks in the plank walls. Ian was still awake. She didn't want to wonder what he was doing. Thinking of him made her miserable in too many ways to count.

She'd been the foolish one to believe in him and to think he didn't look at her and see a good worker or a means to get something for nothing. Fresh fury flowed through her, growing stronger with each wave. So huge she became tall with it, strong with it. She curled her fingers around the smooth wood handles of the satchel so hard her knuckles burned. Anger made the pounding behind her cheekbone worse as she laid her ear to the door. Conversation floated through the ill-fitted boards.

"I don't like it, either, Maeve. But we're better off than we were. We might not have the money, but we more than likely will get to keep the house and get a strong back to work around here. It's the best offer we're gonna get, considering she ran off the one man who would pay more."

"That girl cost us a good opportunity."

"And I won't be forgettin' it."

She wrapped a bubble around her heart to protect it from her parents' words. She eased the satchel to the floor, packed and ready to go. All she needed was to wait for her parents to go to bed and Ian's light to go out. The night silenced, as if waiting, and the enormity of what she was about to do frightened her. This was not her plan, running away when there was no train to whisk her away quickly and without enough money to see her far. Her stinging cheek and throbbing head reminded her of how serious it was to be alone in the world. If Ian had not come along—

She blinked back the hot wetness in her eyes. She was not a girl given to crying or sentimental foolishness. She did not feel anything more than a distant gratitude for the man—really, and if that wasn't the truth, then it would be. She would think of all his faults until this confused need to like him disappeared. She would do everything she could to forget the apology in his eyes back in the kitchen. It wasn't working. Beneath her anger wasn't really hatred at all, but recognition. They were two like souls, one who had lost his dreams and one who intended to find hers.

All she wanted was a safe place to thrive. *It has to be out there somewhere, right, Lord?* The prayer rose up from the truest part of her spirit, from the place within her that no one could break. *Please lead me toward it tonight. Please stay with me so I am not alone.*

The sky outside stretched as if to infinity, the darkly shining prairie vast. Although the storm had stopped, frost hazed the edges of the window panes, a sign of a bitterly cold night ahead. She had dressed warmly in three layers of woolen long johns. Surely that would see her through until morning. She did not know how far she would get, but if she and Flannigan rode until dawn they would be far enough that no one—not even Ian—would come after them.

Time crept slowly until the voices downstairs silenced and the light in the barn faded. *This is it, Fiona.* She rose, gathering her courage. In the inky darkness, she seized her satchel, eased open the door and crept down the ladder. Her father's muffled snoring from the next room told her the faint creak of the boards had not wakened him. She tiptoed across the icy floor, hearing every loose board. Her rustling skirts and the whisper of her movements echoed in the small, dark kitchen.

Almost there. She took her shoes in hand and her wraps from the wall peg and faced her biggest obstacle: the lean-to door. The latch caught, and she laid her coat over it to muffle the sound. The door creaked open— she moved it slowly, inch by inch, until she could squeeze through—and then eased it closed. The latch clunked like a shot in the night. Her pulse stopped. But when she leaned her ear against the door, her father's steady snoring continued to drone.

Whew. Teeth chattering, she slipped into her coat, cinching the sash tightly, and sat down to yank on her shoes.

Small hope steadied her as she waded through the luminous snow. Moonlight shone like a dark pearl, guiding her way to the still barn. Only one hurdle left—she surely hoped Ian was a sound sleeper. She opened the door with care and hoped the rush of icy wind would not be enough to wake him. She waited a moment until her eyes adjusted to the thick darkness.

Down the aisle, the horses dozed. Their rhythmic, heavy breathing was a dependable cadence that hid the light pad of her shoes against the hard-packed earth. She set her satchel near the bottom rung and gripped the thin wood slat. The wood creaked faintly as it took her weight. A small sound, hardly noticeable. She eased her foot onto the ladder rung and climbed to the next board. One step closer to her freedom.

"Where are you going, lass?" A voice rumbled like thunder out of the night. Ian McPherson, not asleep, not at all.

Chapter Ten

Her hand slipped, she lost her balance and her feet hit the ground. The shock of the hard landing traveled up her bones. It was nothing like the shock at seeing him emerge, hands fisted, brawny shoulders set, a man twice her size and strength. He could easily stop her.

"You wouldn't be heading up into the loft to get your running-away money, would you?" His footsteps marched closer, uneven and with the accompanying tap of his cane. "That wouldn't be a satchel at your feet, would it?"

"I'm not interested in having a conversation with the likes of you." Not only had he traded her future for his, he was going to stop her chance to escape. Would he drag her back to the house and her father?

Probably. But instead of grabbing her, he stopped. The lantern well eked open. He was taking the time to strike a match instead of stopping her. He must think she would be too afraid to run now. Or, more likely, that he had her trapped. Well, she was not so easy to defeat. She seized the handles of the satchel, slid them over one wrist and leaped onto the ladder. Rung by rung she rose into the rafters as the match struck and flared, casting light into the darkness like hope, a hope she would not lose.

She could still get away. She felt the pull of his gaze as she tossed her satchel into the hay and tumbled onto the loft boards. She glanced over her shoulder—a mistake. He was a striking sight, bathed in the flicking orange light. Standing tall in that square-shouldered way of his, he appeared to be all that was good and right. A strange glow within her caught and came to life like a flame to a wick. Her eyes teared and she could not explain it. She did not like this man. In fact, she detested him. Ian McPherson pretended to be something he was not. Lying, when he ought to have told her the truth. Befriending her and telling her she was safe with him, when he ought to have admitted he was using her. He was a man she could never trust again.

She had to do her best not to forget that. She hated the wish rising up within her. Foolish, that's what her feelings were. A schoolgirl's stubborn clinging to a fairy tale, one which could never be true. She wrenched away, stinging in deep places she had never known before—yes, she cared about him and her heart knew it. But her mind was more rational and smarter than her heart. She climbed to her feet, determined.

"What are you going to do, Fiona? Run off into the night? Walk down the road all the way to town by yourself?" The sincere concern layering his rich baritone chased up the ladder after her. "You have no protection. Tonight you saw a bit of what can happen to a young lady alone in this world."

"I doubt Da's friend is waiting outside the barn." She scrambled over the beam, catching her hem in her haste. She winced at the ripping sound and dropped to her knees in the sweet, fragrant hay.

"No, but there are plenty of men of his ilk in the world. Do you want to risk being trapped like that again? Or worse? Anything could happen to you. Lass, you do not know how much worse you could be harmed."

How did he get the perfect ring of caring into his tone? She marveled, pawing away shanks of dried grass. He was attempting to play on her fears, on the truth neither of them could deny. Was it smart to run off on her own in the dark? No, but it was better than the known danger here—the danger of losing her freedom and her dreams. She swept off the burlap and pried it off the floor, working as fast as her fingers could go.

"I'm asking you to stay. I'll keep you safe. I won't let any harm come to you. I vow it, on my honor."

Why did her emotions respond? What was wrong with her? She pried up the boards with a clatter. Why did she want to believe his concern was real? He was simply pretending he cared. That was the real Ian McPherson. Sure, he was sorry he had hurt her, but it hadn't stopped him. Now he was trying to talk her out of leaving for his own sake, not hers.

She hardened her heart and dug out the box. Wasn't it odd that Ian wasn't coming up after her? Why wasn't he trying to stop her? There was no telltale squeak of the ladder, no groan of wood beneath his weight.

"I know what you think of me, Fee, and I'm sorry." His voice came from down below at the ladder's base where he waited for her. "Come down and let me take care of you. Let me tell you what I've planned."

She hesitated, brushed by moonlight, feeling the luminescence against her cheek, and it was like the emotion within her, longing to be cared for. But that was only another one of her foolish notions and she could not give in to it. She hated that her fingers trembled too hard to open the box on first try, and it felt as if a sob lodged in her throat. Why did she feel torn apart? What was he doing to her? The sincerity in his tone, the affection in his words were like an unimaginable treasure that lured her; it was what she wanted most. But he was not a man she could trust.

She wedged open the lid. It was too dark to see. Her pulse fluttered wildly. Was her money gone? She bit her lip, forced her hands to stop shaking and held the box up to a slat of moonlight slanting between the boards.

The sock was still there, the contents of the box untouched, the locket glinting faintly in the starlight. What a relief. She grabbed her stash of money, and there was the picture he had drawn. An illustration of a girl and her horse, but on this night she saw something more. The swirl of the wind-driven snow, the stretch of the unseen prairie, the spirit of freedom that somehow came from lashing lines of ink on a page. Almost as if he understood. As if he knew her spirit's longing.

And if he knew that, surely he would understand. She had to leave. She stuffed her savings into the top of her satchel, the hay crackling beneath her step. "I have an offer to make you, McPherson."

"Do tell." A smile crept into his tone; he thought he had won.

She crept deeper into the mow. He still waited for her to come down the ladder. He must think there was no other way out of the barn. It did not feel right to trick him, but then wasn't that what he had done to her? A few more paces brought her to the loading door. "You stay here with the land, and I'll go where I please. Da will be rid of the expense of me, and you won't be forced to marry to get what you want."

"Is that what you think? That I am using you to get the land?"

"Why else would you accept Da's offer?" She shouldered open the heavy door and prayed no boards would creak.

"Have I said a single word about marriage?"

"Not directly."

"And surely you do not think there will be a wedding tonight or tomorrow?"

"Not if I can help it."

"Then why the rush to leave? You will be safe here, lass. This is your home."

"And you're using *this* for an argument?" The icy air felt welcome against her face. She gripped the rope and gave it a testing tug. "I've been hurt enough here. I shall take my chances in that big, dangerous world you are afraid of."

"Do you know what a boardinghouse costs by the week? What of your meals? What if you have trouble finding work? What will you do then? Your savings isn't enough. It won't see you far." Caring rang like a true bell, perfect in pitch and honesty.

A part of her longed to stay, if only for the promise of caring in his voice. As much as she longed to be truly cared for, she did not trust it. The rope held, so she transferred her weight. The door swung closed, bashing her in the shoulder. She bit her lip, ignored the pain and dug her shoes into the hemp. She had to stop thinking of Ian. She inched downward, gritting her teeth as the door bashed her again. She caught it and waited a beat, easing it closed with what she hoped was the smallest of sounds. How long would it take for him to figure out she was gone?

Probably not long. She tossed her satchel. It landed with a muted thump in the soft remnants of hay left over from the morning's feed. The platinum moonlight focused on her like a beacon so she went fast, sliding some of the way, going hand over hand the rest. No time to waste. She hit the ground, grabbed her satchel and ran. Was Ian still talking at her, waiting for an answer? Still trying to convince her that marriage was the best of her choices?

Her breath rose in white clouds as she skidded to a stop at the first stall door—Flannigan's. All she had to do was to release the latch, and the horse would come running. She'd catch a handful of mane, swing up onto him and they would be off, following the call of the prairie and the lure of the moon. She would be free.

A footstep crunched in the snow behind her—Ian, larger than life and radiating fury. She stared at him, disbelieving. Was that really him and not a figment of her fears?

"Going somewhere, lass?" His anger boomed in the empty corral, resounding against the flawless night.

"How did you—"

"I've done the same a time or two when I was a boy." He wrenched the gate open and pounded into the silvered light. Every strong line of his powerful form and the curves of his muscles were highlighted; he looked like a knight of old, mighty and invincible—a very angry knight. "I'm not as dim-witted as you think."

The stars faded; the moonlight waned. Maybe that was simply her hopes hitting ground. She could run, but how far would she get? A few beats of his step and his hand curled around her nape, holding her captive by her coat collar and ending all possibilities.

"Come back inside." His command was not a harsh one.

"I cannot."

"Planning on staying here in the corral all night, are you?" He did not relent, his grip on her steadfast. "You have to go somewhere or you will freeze. It may as well be with me."

"You could let me go." She turned in his grasp, enough to show the plea in her eyes.

Such immense sadness. It was what had struck him hardest about her.

"If I did, do you even know where you would go?"

"Far away as fast as I can."

"That's no sound plan." It pained him to say so.

"I had a good one, but you ruined it." Defiance painted her like the moonlight. "And that means you owe me. Please, Ian, walk away."

A smart man would not care so much. A wise man would lock away his feelings and never let them see light again. He felt sorely alone, although they stood together in the platinum night. "I cannot."

"I could give you half my money. It's not much, but it's something. To just look the other way while I ride Flannigan."

"No." The thought of her alone in this world destroyed him. He reached deep inside for the courage to hurt her more and tugged her toward him. "You must stay with me, lass."

"There has to be something you want, some bargain we can agree to." She dug in her heels. The frost clung to her dark hair and lashes, making her look like some lost winter sprite of ancient lore, a sweet bit of goodness too fragile to be captured for long. "You said we were friends, Ian. If you ever meant that, if you have any honor at all, then close your eyes and when you open them again, I'll be gone. It won't be your fault. You won't know where I am. Please. I can't do what you're asking."

"You're going to have to find a way to, my friend." He softened his words, wanting to make her defeat easier. He did not like the agony taking her over inch by inch—the slump of her shoulders, the tuck of her chin and the way she drew inward just a little. Aye, but she was killing him as surely as if she held a dagger to his heart.

He watched her gulp, watched fear flicker across her face. She came with him haltingly, her feet seeming heavy. For one moment the rebellion remained etched on her like starlight on the wild, endless prairie; the wind lashed her dark curls as if trying to blow her away from him. She was calculating her chances of escaping him, no doubt, measuring the dark corners of the corral and wondering if she broke his hold could she outrun him?

"If you run, then I would be out the money I promised your father. It's in a lawyer's trust in Newberry." He hefted her along, gently but firmly, and prayed his soft—and secret—feelings did not show. "I had a contract drawn up. Fortunate it was there was an attorney in town with the spare time to help me."

"Yes, lucky you." She choked back a sob, but he felt it roll through her, pure agony as if straight from her soul.

He was sorry for it. "It was Providence watching over you, lass. Your father's back payments and fees will be paid, so that you won't lose your home come month's end."

"I intend to lose my home just the same. You can't keep me here, Ian. You can't watch over me every second."

"That's not my wish." He hauled her through the gate, leaving it open rather than release his hold on her. Not because he feared her escape but because he liked holding her close. Being at her side, knowing he was what stood between her and sorrow, knowing he could give her what she wanted most—he and no other man—made his sadness easier to abide. He loved the girl, aye. It was the first blush of emotion but it was love all the same—a love she would never feel for him.

"I sold my saddle," he confessed as they crossed the yard together. "I pawned my grandfather's pocket watch and gold fob, which he gave me for my sixteenth birthday.

Both had been his father's. I had hopes of giving them to my son one day."

"And why are you telling me this? Using guilt to keep me here?"

"I only want you to understand my sacrifice." The path the moon made on the snow felt blessed, extraordinary, as it glittered and gleamed at their feet. Hard to believe there could be any shadows on a night like this, and ones so deeply dark. "I sold my riding coat, the one my grandmother sewed for me before her hands were crippled with arthritis. I found a buyer for Duchess's unborn foal. I did all of that so no man would come along and try to hurt you. Try to break you."

Looking as lost as the shadows, she trembled once, as if she were hesitating, as if she were remembering what had almost happened this night. He saw the strength of it as her chin dropped, and she remained unbowed and unmoving. Not fleeing, after all.

"If I betrayed you, then it was for a good reason." The house loomed above them, silent and still, blocking out a chunk of the star-strewn sky. He nudged her toward the back steps. "You will stay, Fiona. Let's get you back inside."

He ignored the choke of a sob catching in

her throat. His grip didn't relent, nor did the unhappiness burrowing like the cold into his chest. Although they walked side by side, a great divide separated them. One he feared could never be crossed.

"I was wrong about you." Her voice was strained, her words tight with defeat. "You are a much more horrible man than I thought."

"You would not be the first to say so." He wished he knew how to shield his heart better, to turn off his feelings so that he did not care, so that nothing could hurt him. Impossible. Fiona O'Rourke had stripped him bare of armor and shields, leaving him defenseless. As he tugged her through the last of the incandescent snow and into the house's shadow, he had to face the truth. Few things in life hurt as much as Fiona's hatred for him.

Why the kitchen? That's what Fiona wanted to know. This small, unhappy room symbolized everything she feared most. Her mother spent most of her life in this room.

Although the cook stove was cold, the scent of the night's supper and the cigar smoke from Da's card game stained the air. In the corner stood the washboard and tubs, the broom, cleaning buckets and dish basin, reminders of all the unhappy hours here doing chores. It was not the work that troubled her, but the lack of choice. That was what happened when a woman married a man who dominated her.

"Sit here." His order could have been gruff. It should have been. Anger or something similar to it tensed the muscles in his jaw and delineated the angles of his cheekbones. His grip on her arm ought to have been bruising—she knew, for Da had hauled her into the house countless times—but it was not. He drew a chair away from the table and eased her into it. "Don't move."

"You're comfortable giving orders. I suppose this is a hint of how you would treat a wife?"

"Aye." Grim, as if fighting smoldering rage, he set her satchel on the small counter and knelt before the stove.

At least he admitted it. He could have lied to her. She straightened her spine and ignored the burn of her vertebrae against the unyielding wood. She hurt everywhere. Her head, her shoulder, her ankle, her soul.

"Here. Put this against your cheek and hold it there." He pressed something cold into her hand. A cloth wrapped around chunks of ice from the water bucket. "I've never seen a woman climb a rope like that."

"Technically I wasn't climbing. I was going down."

"Aye, but it was hand over hand. Same difference." Towering over her, he looked as stalwart as a legend and twice as difficult to defeat. "Did your brother teach you that?"

"Who else?" For the life of her, she could not be nice to him.

"You two were close?" His hand curled around hers to press the ice tenderly against her cheek. Her wide eyes pinched, and he felt the answering emotion within his chest, as if her grief were his own. "I guess that's obvious, too."

"Johnny was the only real family I had. My folks…" She said nothing more. She didn't have to.

"That's not the way parents are supposed to be." It felt as if they were the only two people on earth, for the silent night and his affections were vast. He pushed away from her. "My grandparents had the real thing. Enduring love and respect and devotion to one another that strengthened day by day. An inspiring sight to see, and a soft comfort to grow up in."

"Surely you want to find the same thing one day."

"Lass, I know what you are about to say." The lamp casing creaked as it opened. "You are hoping I will break my agreement with your father and go off to find such a love."

"Why not? You will not be happy with me, and here? There is no happiness in this home."

"Your reasoning will not work with me." The flare of a match caressed his stony features. "I'm not staying to find happiness."

"I don't understand you, McPherson."

"Aye, this I know." He did not turn from the stove. "You told me that if you wanted something better than your life here, you had to work for it. What would that be?"

"And I should tell you?"

"Why not? I'm curious." A cup rattled in a saucer as his gait whispered near. He leaned close, bringing with him the scent of winter snow and hay and the musty wool of the old coat he wore.

Not the same one he'd arrived in. He had been telling the truth. She spotted a small tear in the collar seam and a patch on the elbow. The ironware clinked against the tabletop, and the warm scents of honey and chamomile curled against her nose.

"That will warm you." He brushed a lock of hair from her forehead, his touch as gentle as a blessing, his kindness unmistakable. "You need another bit of ice for that bump."

"I don't need your pity, McPherson."

"It's not my pity you have."

She did not want his kindness, either. She wanted to hate him. She wished she could see him as the enemy he was. Taking her money as handily as he wanted to take her freedom. And yet, as she listened to him breaking more ice in the water bucket, and the glasslike tinkle as he gathered it into a dish towel, strangely tender emotions glowed within her like banked embers. With any luck, her affection for the man would turn to ash and darkness.

"When I was a little girl sent to my room without any supper, I would close my eyes and dream. Not of storybooks and romance, like I know my friends did, but of the house I would have when I was grown." She didn't know why, but the truth swept out of her. Ian, as if he saw and heard only her, came toward her with an intense focus that both frightened and calmed her.

"I suppose this was a fancy house?" He grabbed an empty chair by the rung and hauled it over, facing her. "Did your grandmother tell you of McPherson Manor, then?"

"My future home was not a fine place, but simple with four walls and plenty of windows to let in cheerful sunshine." She took a sip of the steaming brew, savoring the sweet, liquid comfort. It warmed her and she went on. "It was a place with flowers surrounding it, so that when the wind blew, the whole house smelled like lilacs and roses. It was a place where I was and always would be safe. There was no strap hanging from a nail on the wall."

"And you were in this house alone?" He laid the ice against her temple. "So you could not be hurt?"

How did he know? She blinked hard, for the ice stung, but something secret and deep within her smarted more. "I would have to work hard and save my earnings to afford my own place."

"You hope to find work sewing?"

"Why not? Miss Sims has promised I can use her for a reference. She is pleased with my work. And before you say it, such work might be hard to find right off. I would be happy to do laundry in a hotel or wash dishes in a busy kitchen. I know I can find a job."

"It is winter, and few are hiring this time of year. Did you consider that?"

"You're still not going to let me go?"

"Not on my life."

"You said you would help me."

"And so I am."

You're imagining tenderness in his words, she told herself, knowing it could not be true. And she did not want it to be. Look at the proof of his character as he opened her satchel, removed her money stash and stuffed it into his coat pocket. Warm when he could be cold; mellow when he could be commanding.

"Is there anything more I can do for you tonight?" he asked, as if he cared about her answer.

What she wanted, he would not give her. Exhaustion crept into her like a heavy fog; the numbness of the evening was wearing off. Her head throbbed. Her cheek pounded. Every muscle she owned felt strained and sore. "No, there's nothing I want from you."

"Then up you go." He carried her satchel to the base of the ladder. He waited in silence while she gripped the rungs in her cold hands, realizing she still wore her mittens and coat. She didn't want to spend the few moments it would take to remove them in Ian's presence, so she climbed into the cold attic and darkness. The moonlight had vanished: perhaps clouds were moving in.

"I'll see you in the morning, pretty girl." He tossed her satchel into her hands, and something about the man pulled at the deepest places within her. As if it were her soul that longed after him, wishing for what could not be.

As his uneven gait padded softly through the house, she heard a muted grunt of pain. The kitchen door creaked closed, leaving her alone. She wanted to hate him, but she could not.

Chapter Eleven

"Fiona? Yoo-hoo."

"That must be some daydream."

"About Lorenzo, no doubt. She's smiled the whole time I've been talking about him."

Lorenzo? Fiona frowned, pulled herself out of her thoughts. The cold night—last night—frothy with snow and moonlight vanished from her mind, and she was sitting in the warmth of Lila's pretty parlor filled with sunshine, as she did every Friday afternoon. She poked her needle through the seam of the dress she was basting. Ian might have taken her savings, but she intended to keep earning. Her amused friends were staring at her. Scarlet's grin stretched ear to ear, and Lila covered her hand with her mouth to keep from laughing out loud.

"He does cause a girl to dream, doesn't he?" Kate was busy sighing in agreement. "I don't blame Fee a bit."

"Neither do I." Always faithful, Earlee looked up from threading her needle. "Now that her engagement is broken, why shouldn't she start to consider the possibilities?"

Goodness, was *that* what they thought? That she was daydreaming about Lorenzo courting her? Heat stained her cheeks. What did she say? If she denied it, then it would only make them disbelieve her more. And in truth, she *had* been thinking about a man. Ian—to be precise. But she had *not* been smiling. She was nearly sure of it.

"Look, she's blushing. It's cute," Kate cooed, going back to her embroidery work. "Fiona's first crush."

"It had to happen sometime," Lila said as she studied her hem work. "It may as well be Lorenzo. Every girl in school has gone sweet on him at one time or another."

"He *is* a perfect tenor." Scarlet looked enraptured; having missed paying attention to the story of church caroling practice, this was news to Fiona.

"Plus, he is perfect." Lila sighed airily in agreement.

"Lorenzo and Fiona would make a good couple, don't you think?" Trouble twinkled in Earlee's eyes. "I know you don't want to marry, Fee, but that could change, now that you have a choice."

"Uh, there's really something I need to tell you all." Really, she had to stop them before they began planning her and Lorenzo's wedding. Honestly. She rolled her eyes at the thought. "He came back."

"The Kentucky guy?" Lila put down her needle. "He came back for you and you didn't tell us?"

"You didn't say *one* word. All day at school? All day long?" Scarlet chimed in.

"You could have told us, Fee," Kate added gently.

Why, exactly, was her face feeling hotter? She had to be blushing furiously because her nose was as red as a berry. This was why she'd been afraid to say anything. Even her closest friends would misunderstand the situation and see in Ian's return something that could never be. Why did he have to come back? Why did he have to decide their broken-down farm was so important to him? He should have simply kept going east, back to wherever he belonged. That's what he should have done.

And, if he hadn't, then what terrible thing would have happened? She wouldn't have been able to fight off Da's friend for much longer, although she would have tried her hardest. Ian had saved her from unspeakable things. She felt a needle prick through her thimble, and the sharp sting reminded her of where she was. Maybe she ought to pay better attention to her sewing.

"I understand, some things are too personal to say out loud." Earlee knotted her thread with care. "Ian must be a very special man."

Special? Her tongue tied, and she realized she might as well tell the whole truth. How Ian had taken her savings and forced her to stay. How confusing his kindness to her was, how nice his protection. This morning, all the barn work had been done by the time she'd come downstairs. Her parents hadn't scolded her once as she helped with the kitchen chores. She stared down at her work, at the luxurious velveteen fabric Miss Sims had entrusted her with, and realized her stitches were crooked. How had that happened? She hadn't stitched so badly since she was six years old.

"But private or not, we're your friends," Lila pointed out lovingly.

"Your *best* friends," Kate emphasized.

"You're obligated to tell us." Scarlet leaned forward, eager for the real story.

"We care about you, Fee," Earlee sympathized. "I'm sure you will tell us when you're ready."

"I just might never be ready to talk about *him*." She couldn't even say his name. Her vision blurred—with fury or confusion, she didn't know which—as she took her needle and began ripping out her stitches.

"She's blushing harder," Lila reported.

"How romantic." Kate's voice was pure glee. "Look at her, ready to deny it. But it *is* romantic."

"It's like something out of a novel." Scarlet set down her hoop. "Grandparents who were friends make a solemn vow their grandchildren one day will marry. When hero and heroine meet, they take a fancy to one another and live happily ever after."

"You're like a fairy tale, Fee." Kate sighed. "Earlee could pen a story about you."

"It would be a story with a joyful ending," Earlee agreed. "With love triumphant."

"It is an arranged marriage. Trust me, there

is nothing romantic about that." The thread snapped. Fiona glared at the frayed edges and realized she'd been using far too much force. It was all Ian's fault, because she had been thinking about him. Now she was talking about him. How had he come to dominate her life so fast and thoroughly?

"Lila?" Mrs. Lawson, Lila's stepmother, rapped her knuckles lightly against the open parlor door. "It's four o'clock. Kate's father and Fiona's beau are outside waiting to take them home."

"My *what?*" She couldn't believe her ears. Mrs. Lawson smiled decorously as if nothing could possibly be wrong.

"Your beau." Scarlet winked. "Who would have thought you would be the first of us to have a young man walk you home?"

"No one is more surprised than me." She tucked her needle into the remnants of the seam and folded her work neatly, but she didn't stand up to shrug into her wraps with the same speed as everyone else. She was in no hurry for the pleasant hour to end. Not only had this been the best time of her whole week, but Ian was outside waiting for her. Already wanting control of her, no doubt.

"Next week is our Christmas party," Lila

reminded everyone as they clambered down the staircase. "Can everybody stay longer for supper?"

"I can, but then I live two streets over." Scarlet pushed ahead, leading the way past the back door to the mercantile to the alley entrance instead. "Kate, you have the farthest to come."

"It depends on the weather." Kate paused in the vestibule to pull on her hood. "If there's no blizzard, then yes. I'm sure Pa will let me. What about you, Earlee?"

"I'll just make a meal ahead. I know Beatrice will warm it in the oven and get the food on the table for everyone." Earlee wrapped her muffler around her neck. "Will your pa let you come this time, Fee? You can't miss our last party."

"Da is awfully mad at me." She tugged at her muffler. "I don't know if I will be able to come."

Everyone fell silent. What was there to say? Her friends knew well her father's disposition. Scarlet opened the door and led the way into the brisk air. The magenta blaze of the sinking sun turned the typical small town into a breathless wonderland, like a picture in a children's Christmas book. The snow in the alley gleamed like a rare opal. The violet light dusted the store buildings and the man waiting by a single horse-drawn sled. Sure, there were others in the alley, but all she noticed was the tall, stalwart shadow, radiating integrity so substantial it could be felt and seen in the ethereal light.

"Who is *that?*" Lila breathed.

"Is it *him?*" Scarlet whispered.

Ian. Something strange was happening to her. Her throat had closed up, and it was as if she had forgotten how to breathe. She stammered, unable to say yes or no.

"That's your betrothed?" Kate's jaw dropped.

"He's the one you were supposed to marry? He's the one you were dreading all this time?" Earlee's whisper was a hush of astonishment. "He's utterly well—"

"Handsome. Incredible. Manly," Scarlet finished as if in awe. "No wonder you are letting him court you. That is a man a girl can dream on."

"I didn't think any fellow could be cuter than Lorenzo, but I was wrong," Lila agreed.

"I'm so glad he came back for you." Earlee squeezed Fiona's hand. "How romantic."

"Utterly," Kate agreed.

Lila sighed as if too overcome to speak.

Could anyone have better friends? They were happy for her, thinking the boy she'd dreaded meeting all these years might actually be a once-in-a-lifetime kind of man. From their perspective, she knew that's how Ian looked with those granite-cut shoulders and striking good looks. But he ambled closer, the tap of his cane easy and his reserved smile friendly, and there was no time to tell her friends the truth. That this was no romantic match, and Ian had not returned because of his affections for her. She felt like a miserable fraud.

"Ladies." Ian tipped his wide-brimmed hat, exposing thick dark locks that only enhanced his manliness.

Not that she was noticing such things. Fine, maybe she was, but only as a casual observation. She could not forget what he had done to her.

Her feet stumbled forward and she was aware that her friends were curtsying in greeting, but all she wanted to do was to push him away and out of her sight. He had no right walking into her life like this. He was supposed to be at the farm, perhaps riding the fields, proud of his soon-to-be acquisition.

"Why are you here?" She didn't mean to sound sharp. The words simply came out that way.

"I was in town and about to head home. When I realized the time, I figured I would stop by." He didn't seem perturbed by her tone, not at all. "It would save you the walk."

"I would rather." Oh, she knew what he was up to. Asserting his authority over her, as if she was one of his horses. "Besides, Earlee and I walk part of the way together."

"Then I would be happy to have your friend join us. The wind is kicking up. It's bound to be a mighty cold hike."

"I'm used to walking in the cold. It doesn't bother me. In fact, I prefer it." Her chin hiked up; she couldn't help it. She felt her friends' curious glances and, in Lila's case, a shocked look. More misery filled her up. This man was already making her sound like her mother.

Instead of getting angry, like Da would have done, instead of putting her in her place or shaming her in front of her friends, Ian shook his head. His rich chuckle was like to warm the chill from the twilight air.

"Whatever you want suits me just fine, lass. I thought you would prefer to take a ride behind Duchess. I was going to let you drive her, but maybe another time. If you change your mind, let me know. Nice to meet you, ladies." With a gentlemanly tip of his hat, he turned and strode away, his boots crunching in the icy snow.

"Fiona!" Scarlet whispered, scandalized. "Look at his horse. It's the nicest one I've ever seen."

"Much finer than ours," Lila agreed. "Meredith's family's horses, as amazing as they are, couldn't hold a candle to that one."

"Plus, your Mr. McPherson is quite dashing." Kate gave her a nod. "I would say yes."

"I don't mind walking on my own." Earlee gave her a shove. "Go ahead. You can tell us all about it before church on Sunday."

They all meant well. Fiona studied each dear face, shining with happiness and hopes for her. With McPherson watching, there was no way she could explain. Nor was there time to.

"C'mon, Earlee." She grabbed her friend's hand and tugged her along. "You're not walking home alone in the dark, and Ian's right. It's getting colder by the minute."

"I don't want to intrude." Earlee dragged her feet and looked to everyone else for help.

"Go with her!" Scarlet ordered. "Or she won't say yes to him."

"Have fun, Fee!" Lila called out.

"Your beau will have to bring you early to church!" Kate had reached her father's sled and was beaming. "Don't let him forget."

Oh, he wasn't about to. She could see that as plain as the grin on his face. That dimpled grin, the one that made the setting sun fade in the sky and the earth fall away from beneath her shoes. Proof that the man had entirely the wrong effect on her. She was determined to keep him well away from her heart. She wouldn't stop trying until she had accomplished that goal.

"Wait, Fee." Ian stopped her, sounding far too happy, more proof he was a scoundrel of the worst sort. Taking delight in her discomfort. Using her friends' good intentions to his own advantage. "Let your friend in first, and then you can sit in the middle."

"Next to you?" She would rather have a tooth pulled. But neither did she want poor Earlee to feel uncomfortable being forced to sit next to a stranger. Well, fine. She waited next to him while he helped Earlee onto the board seat.

"Don't even think about it," she warned

him, jerking her hand away. She did not need his help getting into the odd-looking sled. "Where did you get this?"

"I made it with scraps I found around back of the barn."

"Yes. That explains it." Only Ian would have the finest horse in the county *and* the worst vehicle. She ignored his chuckle as she scooted onto the seat beside Earlee.

"It's sort of cute," Earlee whispered. "It's fun."

"Yes, I'm in stitches I'm having so much fun."

Why did Ian have to laugh—again? This was not funny. Not from her view, anyway. He settled in beside her, his arm pressing against hers. She was safe and protected, and that was completely the wrong way to feel. No, she had to stop these sorts of troubling emotions. This was horrible, she decided. It was like sitting next to a big pillar of immovable steel. If she tried to scoot farther away from him, then she would risk inching Earlee off the end of the seat.

"Good meeting you, Schmidt." He tipped his hat to Kate and her father as they trotted by.

"Hope to see you Monday." Mr. Schmidt

said nothing more and in moments the Schmidt sleigh was out of sight.

What, exactly, had he been discussing with her friend's father? The man was infiltrating her life. How did she stop him? He hauled a folded blanket from beneath the seat and shook it. Rich wool tumbled over her, and somehow it was his caring she felt, warm and strong like a hand curled in hers. She found the hem and stretched out the blanket to full length, making sure Earlee had enough to keep her warm. Ian filled her senses, the pleasant male scent of his skin, the rhythm of his breathing and the rustle of his movements. He was the only color she saw in the twilight world.

She barely remembered to wave goodbye to her friends standing shoulder to shoulder in the alley. The sled jerked forward roughly on the rutted snow. Ian's arm moved against hers as he handled the reins. She didn't want to notice his tensile strength and his kindness when he spoke to his mare. The wind knifed through her with shocking cold and stung her eyes. The street flew by in a blur.

"Why are you seeing Mr. Schmidt on Monday?" Earlee asked as the horse and sled stopped at the busy intersection. "Is it because you plan on taking Fiona to school?"

"I'm hoping to get a job at the mill. Mr. Schmidt said he would put in a good word for me with his boss."

"You're going to find work here, in Angel Falls?" It sounded permanent, as if he was entrenching himself not only in her life but in town. The more he did that, the better the chances were that he would never leave.

"You don't want me lounging around like your father, do you?" Gently, as he did many things, he smiled at her.

"The less you are like Da, the better."

It all made perfect sense. Getting a job showed he was responsible—not that she wanted to see any bit of him in a positive light. She refused to like him, and that was that.

Thank heavens there was a break in the traffic. Ian eased his mare into the bustle. The wind gusted, making it too cold to speak, so they glided down the street, decorated for Christmas, in silence.

"Thanks for the ride." Fiona's friend climbed out of the sled, clutching her bag. "I hope to see you again, Mr. McPherson. If you're a churchgoing man, you might want to come with Fiona on Sunday. We have a fun Sunday School class. There are lots of young people our age—"

"I might like that, thank you." It sounded mighty fine to him. He noticed he was alone in that opinion. Fiona retreated to the far edge of the bench seat, and he felt her horror as simply as if she were still pleasantly against his arm.

"Earlee!" She choked, turning as white as snow. "How could you?"

"I just thought he might want to beau you to church—"

"I'm starting to really dislike that word." She looked as if she were being torn apart, and he knew why. The wind had carried to him her friends' whisperings, and he had heard enough to know they assumed a bond had formed between them.

They were not wrong. On his side, at least. A blind man could see the pretty lady's disdain for him.

"What word? 'Beau'?" Fiona's friend asked innocently. "Oh, I see what you mean. You're right. 'Beau' is the wrong word. You're engaged now. How exciting. I should not tell you this, but I'm going to start a little present for your hope chest. I know you haven't started filling one yet, and you need help before your wed—"

"That is really sweet of you." Fiona looked over her shoulder, and he could read the longing on her face as she searched the shadowed, endless prairie. The falling twilight hid the scattering of houses and barns, making it seem lonely and vacant. As if a person could be lost from her problems there forever. "You are the best friend, Earlee."

"No, *you* are the best friend." The girl bobbed a curtsy in his direction. "Nice meeting you, Mr. McPherson. I hope to see you both on Sunday. Bye, Fee!"

Well aware he was that his intended opened her mouth to argue, but her friend was already trudging up the snowy driveway to a ramshackle shanty, windows glowing like a beacon in the gathering dark. Her brow furrowed as she studied him. The bruise and swelling beneath her eye was like a bayonet to his chest. Tender emotions set his teeth on edge, because he could not brush those unruly curls from her face and caress the bruise away.

"You are staring at me. Why?" She looked ready for a fight, but he was not fooled.

"How is your head feeling?" He gave the reins an easy snap and Duchess stepped out, choosing her own pace in the difficult snow.

"You don't need to pretend you care. Actually, I prefer that you didn't."

How could such a slight lass hold such fierceness? Not cruel and not harsh, but fiery, like a filly who did not want to be bridled. She reminded him of someone, another female he was fond of, although in a very different way.

He guided Duchess around the sharp bend in the road and directly into the raging wind. He couldn't say why he hardly noticed the stinging temperatures. His gaze, his senses, his very essence were glued to her.

"I know you are mad at me." Well he understood, so he did not fault her for it. "I've treated you unfairly, coming back like I did. Bargaining with your father for you."

"For the land," she corrected him. A less attentive man might have missed the deep well of pain beneath the surface of her words. "You don't want me. I'm just the means to land you can't buy any other way."

"And what makes you think that, little filly?"

"Filly? I am not a horse. Have you not noticed?" She whirled to face him, and although the darkness and shadows cloaked her, it was as if he could see the pain on her face, hidden beneath her anger.

He could not argue with her. He shrugged, unable to deny it because he feared to say the wrong thing. He could not make her hurt worse.

"Hard to believe once I *almost* thought you were a decent man. You are much more horrible than I ever guessed. Then you went and took—" She fell silent.

He heard emotion catch in her voice, hurting with her. "You mean when I took your money?"

She did not answer, but he sensed it. Deep inside it was like a door opening, and he could see her clearly in a way he had never perceived anyone before. The shadows tried to hide her as nightfall descended more deeply over the land and over them, but he didn't need light to see that her anger was meant to push him away.

"I'm not like your father, Fiona."

"Maybe, but you seem a lot like him to me." Her disdain was layered, as if it did not come to her easily.

Her opinion of him weighed heavily. He

swallowed the sting in his throat, adjusted the reins into one hand and drew the small packet from his coat pocket. "I'm not completely like the man," he argued.

She didn't answer, but he heard a distinctive harrumph, as if she highly doubted his statement. She had every right to her opinion, but did she have no belief left?

The last of the sunset's blaze disappeared from the underbelly of the clouds, the sky darkened and night fell grim and bleak. The cruel wind moaned, and he could only hope he was doing what God wished. It was hard to tell. He reined Duchess off the main road and onto the narrow drive.

"Here." He held out the small ledger.

"What is it?" She took it, uncomprehending.

"The record of your savings account at the bank. It's in my name, but yours is on there, as well. It is safer than stashing it in the barn. You can keep adding to your going-away fund." He halted them in front of the barn and turned to her with his feelings veiled. "That's what you wanted, right?"

Chapter Twelve

She wished she could see his face to read his emotions. The darkness hid all, making it impossible to see if a lie or the truth shone in his gaze, if he was offering her a dash of hope or taking it away. She clutched the little book tightly. "Is this really mine?"

"Every penny." The winter air vibrated with his honesty.

He hadn't taken her savings. That single thought rolled around in her mind, first with disbelief and then acceptance. The hard shell she'd put around her heart cracked a fraction, leaving vulnerable places unprotected. "But if this is in your name, it is technically yours."

"Aye, by law that would be an argument." The blanket rustled, and his shadow rose as if into the star-strewn sky. "But this way your father cannot touch it, and you can. You can withdraw the full amount any time you wish. This means you can run. I won't stop you, lass."

"You make no sense, McPherson. Last night you dragged me back to the house—"

"Aye, so you would listen to what I'm asking you." His strong, warm hand curled around hers, warm and significant, and held on tight. His fingers twined between hers were companionable, right. As he helped her from the sled, her fear of him began to drain. She landed beside him, defenseless and small. Snow slid over the tops of her shoes, wetting her stockings, but the sudden cold did not steal her breath the way Ian did.

"What are you asking?" she asked.

"To let me help you."

"You want to help me run away from you?"

"Aye, why else do you think I have agreed to stay?" He shouldered open the barn door, waiting for her to enter first. "I intend to help you, Fee. I promise you that."

"And I suppose like any man you think that really means you are helping yourself?"

"I came back for you." As substantial as truth, as intangible as dream, and yet real all the same. "Why else would I have pawned what I had on me, all but my horse, to come back here?"

"It was for the land."

"Which is no prize. It comes with a mortgage a man would have to break his back working to pay off. Surely you must know that."

"Johnny used to talk about it. He said Da was bad with money."

"I am not." He waited, his feet planted, his legs braced, and in the shadows the starlight found him. "I came back to help you find a better life. I do not think I can go on with my own unless I know you are safe and well. Only the good Lord above knows why."

"I almost believe you." Why was he doing this to her? How did he strip her defenses away with a few honest-sounding words?

Only the Lord knew why she was susceptible to him. She wrenched away, having the advantage of knowing the inside of the barn by heart, and moved through the darkness faster than him. The horses whinnied, moving around in their stalls, and the cow lowed in greeting.

"I pity the man who does marry you." Amused now, his brief chuckle rang cozily through the barn. His chest bumped her shoulder blade as he reached around her to take the match tin before she could grab it.

"You mean you pity yourself?" She whirled to face him.

"I do, and the man who wins your heart. For he will fall in love with you so hard and strong he would give up anything for you. And you could crush him with a word and that temper of yours." He struck the match, and the flame worshipped him as he lit the lantern.

Why did he have to be so appealing to her? Why was he tearing her into pieces? When she suspected the worst of him, he proved to be a better man. The small book she clutched felt like a weight on her soul. "I don't understand you. You make no sense."

"I'll not argue with you." He tugged the ledger from her grip. Outlined as he was by the golden, glowing light a more fanciful girl could imagine him the hero of a dime novel, a man who stood for all that was good in the world, who was both unwaveringly tough and endlessly gentle. He folded open the first page of the booklet and tipped it toward the light for her to clearly see.

There was her money, all twenty-three dollars and forty-six cents. Not that she had doubted him. A strange aching emotion built in her throat, something she couldn't swallow past—something she was afraid to look at too closely. Because then she would no longer be able to keep trying to hate him. Now there was no way to keep him safely away from her inexperienced heart.

"Let us make a deal, you and I." His rugged voice vibrated with layers too dangerous to think about.

"I do not make bargains with men of your ilk."

"Perhaps just this one time, for tonight, you can amend that and come to an agreement with me. Better to deal with me than with your da, right?"

"For a man who does not gamble, you know which cards to play."

"As your father says, life is a gamble. I have learned much with the losses I have been dealt." His richly layered words drew both the light and the darkness.

His honesty and sorrow touched her. The earth beneath her shoes tilted—again. She forgot to breathe—again. Every word she knew clumped into an incomprehensible ball in her brain. She hated that he was hurting. What was wrong with her that she wanted to comfort him? She knew sorrow well, and knew, too, that he had lost more than she had ever known. But his betrayal remained, and she could not afford to be kind. "What do you want, McPherson?"

"I want you to stop worrying. You're not alone. Not anymore." Tenderness hid in the layers of voice, a tenderness she must be imagining. "Now that you and I are engaged, at least as far as your father is concerned, he will not be trying to hand you over to the next man who comes along."

"I do not intend to marry you."

"You can go to school, spend time with your friends, sew to your heart's content." He tucked the ledger into her coat pocket. "Hide that. Add to it. When you're ready, I will help you go. Wouldn't it be better if you left with a job waiting and someone looking out for you?"

"I don't need you, McPherson."

"Aye, I see that. But I need you." There he went, tricking her with his tenderness and kindness.

He could not be telling the truth. She backed away from him. "I sincerely doubt that. What about the land? That's why you came and that's why you are saying these things."

"Wrong." He drew himself upright, steeling his spine and setting his jaw. His tenderness vanished, leaving behind a formidable man, one who looked strong enough to defeat any foe. "Fiona, I didn't come back for the land. That was not the true reason I am here. I will vow it on a stack of Bibles if you want me to. I vow it on my honor."

"You don't want to marry me?"

"Now, I never said that. But marriage between us always has and always will be your choice, pretty girl." He cupped her face with the curve of his hand, tenderness real and tangible, not imagined. The sweetest longing spilled up from her soul. Everything within her wanted to believe him. She squeezed her eyes shut, and the image of the man remained etched in her mind. As did the caring chiseled into his stony features, and his concern reaching out as if to rope her in.

When she opened her eyes, he hadn't moved. In his secondhand coat, rumpled shirt and trousers he did not at all look the horrible man he that she wanted him to be.

A friendly meow filled the silence between them. A furry paw reached down from the rafter above and batted at Ian's hat. His buttery chuckle warmed the cold air, and his amusement beat at her falling defenses.

"Hello to you, too," he crooned to the cat. "Come to see if there's any milk, have you?"

Mally's answering meow left no doubt, and while the feline tossed a glance Fiona's way, it was a mere glance, nothing more.

"You have gone and stolen my cat," she accused. "I don't think I shall ever forgive you, Ian."

"At least you are using my first name, lass. It is an improvement." He batted playfully at Mally's paw. The cat, apparently thrilled, grabbed hold of his rafter and reached down to wrestle with Ian properly.

"It's not an improvement. Simply resignation." It was easier to let him think she still loathed him than admit the truth. She grabbed a small pail from the nearby shelf. "As you insist on playing, I'll get started on your work."

"I left Duchess standing in the doorway." He chuckled again, dodging the cat's attempts to knock his hat off. "I'll take care of her, don't you worry."

"You are hardly trustworthy." She let the mare scent her hand. Once the beautiful mare nodded in greeting, she dared to run her fingers over the rich velvety nose. Softer than it looked, she marveled. "You are like the finest satin."

Duchess nickered low in her throat with great dignity and dipped her nose in the bucket. Her lustrous red coat seemed to gleam, as if holding light of its own. Breathtaking to be so close to her. She was perfection. Not the kind of horse you leave standing. No, judging by the perturbed look, Duchess was used to immediate attention. She stomped her foot, not at all pleased to find the bucket empty.

"It's hot water I'll be fetching for you. I suppose you are used to your oats warm," she told the mare, fully aware of Ian coming closer. The nerves on her nape tingled in warning at his approach.

"That would be kind of you, lass." His warm breath fanned across the back of her neck. His hand landed next to hers on Duchess's silken nose. "I have left her too long already. She's used to receiving all of my regard."

"Poor Duchess." Fiona sympathized. "It must be hard to endure so much of Ian."

The mare tossed her head up and down as if in perfect agreement.

"I guess that puts me in my place."

His chuckle followed her out into the bitter cold; she couldn't rightly say she was running from it. Just as it was not his warm, cozy company she would be missing. It was *not* the promise of hearing his laughter again that had her hurrying down the path toward the shanty's glowing window.

At least, that's what she told herself.

A strange power had overtaken him, there was no denying it. Ian ran his hands down Duchess's legs, checking knee and fetlock and hoof. No warm spots, no swelling, nothing out of the ordinary. Everything his grandfather had taught him about horse care was ingrained, and as he lowered the mare's hoof onto his knee to check her shoe, the old man could have been with him, standing as he always did with a bit of advice to offer. Fine when Ian was a six-year-old, but how it had annoyed him as a teenage boy.

Warm memories curled around him like his grandfather's loving presence used to. He almost glanced over his shoulder to see if the older gentleman stood there. Impossible, of course, his grandfather had been gone a full year, but perhaps he was looking down from heaven. And if he was, would he be glad of what he saw? Relieved he was falling for the granddaughter of his best childhood friend? Or would he be ashamed of her circumstances?

Duchess blew out a breath through her lips, a sort of horsey huff. How long had he been kneeling here, with her hoof in his hand? Ian blinked. He had no notion how much time had passed.

"Sorry, girl." He eased her hoof to the ground and straightened. Duchess forgave him with a low, affectionate nicker.

The barn door creaked open, and Fiona waltzed in. He would have liked to say that his every sense wasn't attuned to the woman. But no matter how hard he tried, his ears picked up the light, padding rhythm of her boots on the ground and the rustle of her skirts.

The animals turned toward her. Flannigan whinnied in welcome and the cow lowed mournfully. Even Duchess watched with eagerness, and he was able to rise and brush the straw from his trousers as if he were too busy to notice the change in the air or in his heart. Fiona murmured low to the animals. Her sweet voice could melt the frost on the walls.

Aye, it was a strange influence she had over him, but not an unwelcome one. He laid his hand on his mare's neck to lead her gently, wordlessly to her stall. Duchess trusted him, walking confidently beside him, but her attention, too, remained on the dark-haired dream of a woman in her green gingham dress as she stooped to pet the cat eagerly curving about her heels.

Lord, I am trusting where You lead me, that this will all be well in the end. He had to turn to prayer, because he could not see. It was like standing at a crossroads in the dark. Trails led off in many directions, and there was no way to know what lay ahead or which was the one that would bring him home. There were no dreams here to be had; he had more money to earn if he were to buy the deed from O'Rourke, and that would be no easy path. Fiona despised him, and that would not change. He did not miss the difference in her, now that she understood his cause. She sparkled, her step was light, happiness warmed her voice as she stopped to rub Flannigan's nose and explain the hot mash was not for him. The horse leaned into her touch, closing his eyes. When she skipped away, he leaned after her, yearning for more than he could have.

Aye, he knew how Flannigan felt. The light pad of her step and the scrape of the bucket as it landed on the barrel top—every movement she made glanced through him. He could not say why she was dear to him, only that he was alone in that regard. His feelings would never be returned. Aye, he did not need to be a genius to know this. When he ambled close to her, her brightness dimmed as if she were drawing herself in. Clearly whatever friendship they'd had was damaged. Perhaps beyond repair.

He was sorry for it but not for helping her. Not for what it was costing him. He rested his cane against the side of the grain barrel and watched tension creep into the delicate line of her jaw because of his nearness. She was quick to swirl away and put distance between them.

"Thank you for bringing the water." He prayed no wounded feelings crept into his voice. He pried the lid up and stirred oats into the few inches of water. Fiona had thought to leave a spoon in the bottom of the pail, so he stirred, the scraping filling the silence between them when she did not answer.

Aye, there would be no easy laughter between them again. He was sorry for it, too. More than he ever wanted to admit. He gave the plumping oats a final stir. "I'll finish up the chores if you want to go in where it's warm."

"You have invaded my haven." She scooped up the cat in her arms, cradling him like a baby. "Now I must choose between spending time in the shanty with my parents or out here with you."

"Sounds like a difficult choice, lass." He wagered she might think so. He lifted the pail, crossing the aisle with a limping gait. "I'm sorry if I'm the least of two bad choices."

"You are not the worst choice."

Was that a grin threatening to tug upward at the corners of her mouth? He could not be sure. Maybe it was his hope making him see what wasn't there. He lowered the bucket over the stall gate and held it as Duchess dunked her nose in and lapped at the good food daintily. The other horses pricked their ears and scented the air, straining against their doors, hoping for the same. Flannigan nickered. Riley kicked the wall. The cow mooed sadly.

"Where did you get that coat?" She watched him through narrowed eyes. There was no telling what the lass was thinking, but she made a pretty sight, caressed by the lantern light, her curls tumbling out of her braids and with the cat in her arms.

His fingers itched for his pen and paper. She made a pretty picture, but it was more than drawing her image he yearned for. He wanted to memorize the perfect angle of her cheek, to etch into his soul the sight of her gentle spirit. He was a sorry cause, pining after her so. He focused on the horse in front of him. The mare, done with her oats, licked the bottom of the pail harder and gazed at him with her liquid brown eyes in protest.

"There will be more tomorrow, don't you worry." He rubbed her poll, laughing when she bumped her forehead against his palm, wanting more adoration. He felt Fiona's gaze and the question behind it. "Are you still pitying the horse, lass?"

"Something like it. You two have a deep bond."

"Aye. I helped see Duchess into the world. Her dam was my first horse. I was a boy, hardly school age when my ma and I came to stay with my grandparents. She was my first great responsibility, the gentling and training up of her."

"You did not do too badly."

"Perhaps it was the quality of the horse more than the one who raised her." He could not disguise the pride as he gave his mare one final rub. "She's the best of the best."

"I'll not argue that." She set the cat on the stall railing, and he sauntered away, still purring. Perhaps she watched her feline because it was easier, pretending there was distance between them. "You didn't mention your father. He must have been there, too."

"Pa found being a husband and father difficult. He tried, but he could never settle down." He did not mention the long stretches where they had not known where his father was. How Ma would fret and cry with worry, with no money left to buy bread and staples. How she could cry with heartbreak late in the night when she thought him asleep. He'd been a little guy, but he had been old enough to know his father was a man who loved only himself. "My mother was happier living on the estate, but she died a time later in childbirth."

"I'm sorry. I didn't know you lost your ma." She hesitated outside the bright pond of light, as if unsure to stay away or come close.

"It was a long time ago. The Lord made

sure I was not alone. My grandparents raised me, and I could not have asked for better."

"What about your grandmother? You must miss her."

"Aye. I sent her a telegram but there has been no news in return. I worry about her." He set the bucket on the floor next to others needing to be washed. "She has been frail enough since Grandfather's passing, but she is happy and well cared for."

"Can she travel?"

"The doctor says only by rail. Which poses a problem, as I do not have that kind of cash, unless I sell the rest of what I have."

"Do you mean Duchess?" She eased into the fall of light, knowing she risked him seeing what she feared was on her face—sympathy, no matter how hard she tried not to care at all. "You don't want to sell her because she was a gift from your grandfather."

"I am surprised you can see that much of me."

"It is not that difficult. You are not such a mystery."

"I suppose not." When his smile played across the contours of his mouth, dimples cut into his cheeks. "She is my prize mare, but there are others. I managed to keep a dozen brood mares from the clutches of the creditors."

"They were what you spoke of, the hopes to rebuild what was lost." She didn't know what drew her toward him, only that he fascinated her. He, with his lost hopes and family; she knew what it was like to be left with broken dreams and no one to comfort you. "Is it true what you told me, about selling your things?"

"I have told you nothing but the truth."

"And you are staying to help me when your grandmother needs you, too?"

"When you put it that way, I sound like a terrible grandson." He swiped at a lock of hair falling rebelliously into his eyes. It would be easy to imagine him a prince in a fairy tale, with his handsome charm and steel integrity.

No, she did not think him such a horrible man. Not anymore. Not at all.

"I didn't have it in me to leave you, Fee. Good friends are with Nana, so she is cared for. But you. You have no one to care for you." He stopped, his face growing stony and impossible to read.

"Those things you sold, that could have been money to help your grandmother. Yet you spent it for me." She wasn't aware of crossing the aisle; suddenly she was close enough to feel the weight of his regret.

"I do not feel the money was wasted."

"That coat is terrible. It is worn and patched." She cleared her throat but the emotion remained, revealing.

"It was what I could afford." He did not sound sorry.

"When you come in for supper, leave it in the kitchen." Her chin came up; she stepped back, putting distance between them once more. "I will mend that tear when I'm through with the dishes. You cannot leave it like that. The rip will only get worse."

"That's thoughtful of you."

"No, it is not." Emotions deepened her blue irises, ones that looked both soft and ready to fight him. "If you are going to come to church with me on Sunday, then I cannot have you embarrassing me."

"I understand." He saw that she no longer hated him. It was something. A quiet gift in the silence between them on this cold winter's night. She spun on her heel and took the light with her. When she paused in the doorway, she stole the last pieces of his heart.

"Don't think this changes anything between you and me," she warned.

"No worries, lass."

When she left him alone in the barn, it was without hope. Some loves in life were never to be.

Chapter Thirteen

Ian was shivering. Even through the steady snowfall, she could see him trembling on the other side of the sled seat. Ma sat between them, well bundled and staring straight ahead, not overly concerned about the man driving them to church. She wouldn't be. Ma did not like Ian. Whatever agreement he had reached with Da had not made her parents happy.

But she could not forget how thin the fabric when she had mended the tear in his coat or all that he had told her. *I came back to help you find a better life. I do not think I can go back to my own unless I know you are safe and well. Only the good Lord above knows why.*

The Bible cradled in her hands felt reassuring and troubling at once. Snow lashed at her face, burning her exposed cheeks and nose with its needlelike iciness. But she was comfortable enough in her coat, layers of flannel and wool, and with the old blanket draped over her and Ma for extra warmth. At least her teeth were not chattering as Ian's were. What would the book she held have to say about his sacrifice? Or her hard-set determination against him?

The church sped into sight, its spire reaching up into the hazy snow. Families tumbled out of sleighs or walked along the street toward the church. Little kids, warmly bundled, skipped ahead of their parents, or trailed behind, being gently reprimanded either way. She tried not to notice the patient manner in which Ian directed Flannigan, who was distracted by all the excitement, and the way he guided him to a stop at an available hitching post.

"Ladies." Ian stood to help Ma from the sled. Ma refused his hand with a huff. The way she did it, chin up and a frown darkening her face, was a shocking reminder.

Hadn't she treated him the same way days earlier? Shame filled her. Had she been that coldhearted to him? The man was suffering in the temperatures without complaint. What did it say about him that he offered her his hand, knowing how she felt? Did he expect her to act like her mother again? There was no sign of it on his face as he waited with quiet dignity, palm up.

Surely he deserved better from her. It went against the grain to lay her hand in his, to willingly accept what he offered. It was more than a gentleman's manners, much more, and as his fingers closed around hers, she felt the catch of it deep within her soul, like recognizing like.

I do not want to care for him, she thought, but it did no good. Her shoes sank in the snow and her hand remained tucked in his. Snow sifted around them like grace, like peace everlasting, forcing her to see with the eyes of her heart. How tall and straight he stood, as if no hardship was big enough to break him. His grip on her hand was both binding and reverent, protective but not overbearing as he guided her out of the ice. When he released her, she felt sorely alone although he was a mere foot away, tethering Flannigan's rope.

No, she did not want to care for him, but she did. She cared that he was not dressed well for the frigid morning. She cared that he hid it with a handsome smile. She cared that his limp was more pronounced today. Why had she never asked how he'd been hurt?

He handled the horse with care and competence; Flannigan obediently stood and waited with a swish of his tail. No attempt to fight. No sideways kick. The animal nickered and pressed his nose into the man's touch. Ian double-checked the knot securing Flannigan solidly to the iron ring of the post. "Almost done, boy."

Flannigan nickered, bumping Ian again. Something had changed. The horse no longer tried to bite men. He stood patiently, his defiance gone, swinging his neck to keep an eye on his caretaker as he circled to the back of the sled.

Ian was changing things, changing her. She tucked her Bible into the crook of her arm. While he blanketed Flannigan, working the fastenings and smoothing the wool, she tried not to notice the care he gave the horse, or how handsome he looked with happiness softening the chiseled angles of his face. A born horseman, her grandmother had called him. He surely was that.

"Do you miss your horses back home?"

"Until it hurts. I have cared for them all,

most since they were wee foals." He gave Flannigan one final pat and a promise they would return to him soon. He joined her on the side of the road, where sleighs full of families whirred by on the ice. "They are my best friends."

"I can understand that." She brushed a stray lock out of her eyes.

"I thought you might. Nana always worried about me, growing up in the barn the way I did, always with Grandfather and the horses. She feared I would grow up to be an odd young man, and when we met you would refuse to marry me."

"Wise woman, your nana. She was right."

"Hey!" Their laughter mingled together, sweet and a perfect chord. "There's a clearing in the traffic. Careful of the ice."

"I have been crossing icy streets for as long as I can remember. I hardly need help from you." Her words could have been cutting, but they weren't. Emotion hid in the layers, soft and shy.

Maybe it was only his wishful thinking. He ignored the wince of pain in his thigh, leaned on his cane and caught her hand with his. "I'm your fiancé. It's my right to help you across the icy street."

"What else are you thinking you've a right to?"

Oh, he caught that flicker of a grin. She was teasing him, for she had no notion how the torch he carried for her could light up the darkest night. He prayed he could keep those feelings hidden. He suspected the lass would have nothing to do with him—even accepting his help—if she knew. They reached the side of the road, but he kept her hand and did not let go.

"Oh, I was thinking I have the right to control your life. Order you around. Get you to do all the barn work." He could tease, too.

"Funny. You are hysterical, McPherson."

"Sure, but I'm serious. I'm taking charge of your life."

"Go ahead and try." She did not seem alarmed. Perhaps because she trusted he would never leave the barn work to her. No, a mischievous sparkle gleamed within her, a hint at her untamable, beautiful spirit. "I'm not sure, but I think I could take you in a fight."

"You would win hands down, lass." His laughter rang out, and pleased he was that they laughed together. Aye, but the girl was good for his weary soul. "I could not fight you."

"Because you are afraid of losing to a girl?"

"Because I would want you to win." The truth slipped out and hovered in the chilly air between them. He winced, afraid she could hear what he did not want her to know. The churchyard was up ahead, and the crowd that went with it. The cheery rumble of conversations broke the silence that fell between them.

He watched her out of the corner of his eye, wondering if she could guess, if he had been too revealing. He steeled his spine, ready to take the hit if she figured it out and very plainly and fairly rejected him, as he knew she would do.

"Fee!" A familiar voice called out above the hustle and bustle of the busy street. One of her school friends, the one whose family owned the mercantile.

"It's Fiona!" The second girl, the one with the red hair, joined the first one, waving from the snowy churchyard.

"And you brought your beau." The third girl, Mr. Schmidt's daughter, looked so happy she couldn't stand still.

Oh, he saw exactly what they thought. They wanted Fiona happy. As he crunched to a stop on the snowy path, he realized how things looked. Him and Fiona walking side by side and hand in hand, like other serious young men and women headed to church— courting couples. Fiona must have come to the same conclusion. She dropped his hand and stepped away.

"Ladies." He tipped his hat and did his best to smile, so the lass wouldn't guess how her reaction hurt him. "Good morning. If you will excuse me, I'd like to go in search of the minister."

"His name is Reverend Hadly, and you don't have to leave." A crinkle burrowed across the bridge of Fiona's nose, an ador-able furrow. "We're going down to the church basement. I was going to introduce you to some other fellows."

"Oh, I think we could all do that, Fiona," one of the girls answered, while another whis-pered, "Lorenzo," making the first one blush.

Girls. They were a mystery to him. But the only mystery he was interested in was Fiona. An apology shone in her eyes, true and lus-trous. She hadn't meant to hurt him, and she was handing him a peace offering to join the rest of her friends.

"I will come find you after a bit." He nodded toward the front steps where a line had formed. Mrs. O'Rourke was standing with another severe-looking lady, he noticed, waiting to speak to a white-collared older man. He tipped his hat, leaving Fiona before he had the chance to say more. He wanted to stay with her, but it hurt too much.

"We have a surprise for you, Fee." The girls grabbed hands. "Where is Earlee?"

"She's not here yet."

"Then we'll show her later. C'mon, Fiona."

"Come where? What surprise could you possibly have?"

He could not say why her voice followed him, or why of all the conversations surrounding him, her quiet alto was the one he heard clearly. The line had grown, and he took his place behind an elderly couple. His gaze strayed to the edge of the yard where Fiona was hopping up and down in excitement as another girl, one he had not seen before, joined the group. Their squeals of happiness and welcome made him smile.

"Henrietta, I see your girls are back from their East Coast school." A voice floated to him from farther ahead in line.

"Yes, they arrived on yesterday's train. With that dangerous storm, I feared they might have troubles with snow on the tracks. There was a terrible crash only last month. Thank the Lord the girls arrived safe. I do not like these modern contraptions, but they are convenient. A coach trip would have taken months."

"It's good your family is all together for Christmas," her friend replied.

Christmas was coming. Aye, living on the joyless O'Rourke farm, he had nearly forgotten. But the memories of the blessed season blew through him like a chinook. As the bell in the steeple rang, he remembered the church back home, which he had attended with his grandparents since he was a boy. He would miss Christmas Eve service there this year, cutting a tree for his grandmother, the carols she would play on her beloved piano and the hymns on Christmas Day. He missed home, the ache soul-deep. He longed for what was— the beautiful horses grazing in the green pastures, the sense of rightness as he worked a colt in the paddock and the history of his family on the land, land now gone. Land his grandfather had loved and his grandmother grieved; land he was still hoping to get back.

He was not the only one clinging to the past. He understood more what his grandmother felt. It was not the McPherson name that she wanted to establish, but the moments of love that time stole day by day, that were only memory now. The caring looks Nana and Grandfather had shared over morning tea, across the blooming fields and beside the fire at the end of the day. As the Bible said, all things had a beginning and an end, all things a season. He felt alone as he stood, a solitary man among groups of family and friends.

Across the way, Fiona was hugging another newcomer, a girl in finely tailored clothes. Must be one of the daughters home from the East Coast school, he reasoned, watching as his betrothed hopped up and down with excitement. He had never seen her this happy. A pretty picture she made with her braids bouncing and the skirt of her blue-checked dress swirling around her ankles. Snow dappled her, sweet as sugar. Gone were the shadows, the sadness and the troubles of her daily life. She was bursting with joy; not only could he see the evidence of it, he could feel it deep within. As if his spirit knew hers. His fingers itched to draw her, to try to capture her elusive spark. But the line moved forward, and the kindly minister was offering his hand.

"I'm so pleased to know you," Reverend

Hadly said with great sympathy. "I have worried over and prayed for little Fiona. What a blessing your coming here must be for her."

"I hope so, sir." He shook the minister's hand and when he walked away, he felt something more, something like the notice of God. Nana always said that to find His will, all a person had to do was to look into his heart.

When I do, Lord, I see Fiona.

Her musical voice, wholesome and lovely, stood out from all the others. Aye, she looked her age for a change, laughing and carefree with her friends as girls were wont to do.

Confirmation that the decision he had made was the right one.

Fiona bowed her head for the final prayer, far too aware of the man at her side. The man who seemed to dominate the sanctuary. The man every one of her friends thought was in love with her.

Love? She studied him out of the corner of her eye. With his head down, his rugged face poignant in prayer, he was the perfect image of faithfulness. As if every piece of his soul was focused solely on the minister's prayer for peace and selflessness during this holy season. That's what she ought to be focusing on, too, except her mind could not keep track of what was being said. She concentrated, clearly hearing Reverend Hadly's every word. But did they make any sense? No, of course not. Her brain was like her morning oatmeal, all mush and steam.

"Fiona, stop fidgeting," Ma hissed on her other side.

I'm trying to pay attention, Lord. Even her prayer felt mired down next to the track her mind kept following.

"Look at the way he stared down Lorenzo," Lila had whispered over their Sunday-school table in the basement only an hour before. "Your Ian is serious."

"I'll say. Did you see the way he gazes at her?" Scarlet had to voice her opinion—of course. "He can't take his eyes off her."

"Only to glower at Lorenzo." Kate beamed with happiness, as if that were proof of eternal devotion.

"And the loving way he helped her with her coat and keeps watch over her." Earlee's sigh held with it great romantic hopes.

"He loves her," they all pronounced, practically in unison.

He does not love me, she thought stubbornly. He couldn't possibly. Her friends, as dear as they were, did not know everything. They were slightly unrealistic where romantic love was concerned, bless them. Her stomach twisted up like it did when she was afraid of something. And well it should, because believing something like that would be a big mistake.

Someone touched her elbow and she jumped to stand. Ian.

"Are you all right, lass?" His faint Irish brogue resonated gently.

"Fine." Fine? That was all she could say? She had no trouble speaking her mind usually, except her brain was still oatmeal. She managed to shuffle her feet forward toward the end of the row. It was all her friends' fault for putting these fanciful notions into her head.

She crept forward. The end of the row seemed miles away. Maybe it was because Ian was inches from her back, his six-foot height like a mammoth unwanted mountain behind her. Love, indeed. The man did not love her. Ridiculous idea. That's what came from dreaming about romance all the time— you started seeing it whether it was there or not. Good thing she was not a fanciful sort.

It was why she wanted a future she could depend on, relying only on herself.

Finally, she reached the row's end—escape. She slipped into the crowded aisle only to have Ian's hand land on her shoulder, stopping her.

"You aren't going to stay after and help out?" He leaned close, his chin stirring her hair. Goodness, he was near and far too intimate.

"I have to go home," she confessed, but not the reason for it.

Ma, having heard the conversation, whipped around. "Fiona spends far too much time with those girls as it is. Church is serious, not meant for idle play and garishness. Come along, girl."

"Yes, Ma." Why wasn't Ian following her?

"Don't you want to stay?" Puzzled lines dug into his brow as he leaned on his cane. "You can't help decorate the tree if you leave."

She could see why her friends had drawn the wrong conclusions. He was simply a kind man, and it would be easy to see more if you didn't understand. Ian was faithful; he did what was right. That was why he was helping her. He saw it as the correct thing to do. She liked that about him. Against her will, a wisp of admiration ribboned through her, as airy and pure as the daylight hazing the stained-glass window.

Oh, it was something more than admiration, she admitted. She hardly heard Ma's sharp words of reproach, ordering her to hurry up.

"She will stay if she wants to." Ian's tone brooked no argument, but to her, he was gentle. "I will take your mother home and be back to get you."

"But Da will be mad—"

"I will deal with your father, too." Ian looked a great deal older than his nineteen years. He pressed something into her hand. A twenty-five-cent piece. "I heard the group goes up to town for the noon meal before they start decorating."

She stared at the quarter, but it wasn't the gift that touched her. "You will come back?"

"If you want me to."

"I suppose that would be tolerable."

His smile came slow as sunrise. He tipped his hat before he donned it and took a step away. "Have fun, lass."

The church crowd had thinned out; they were alone in the aisle. Ian turned on his heel and strode away, ever so strong and solitary.

She did not know why she felt his wounds, the depth and breadth of them. She liked the man. Very much. She couldn't help it.

"I can't believe you get to stay." Scarlet's footsteps echoed in the aisle behind her. "Thanks to your Ian."

"This is going to be so fun, Fee." Lila grabbed her hand.

"And to think, he's coming back." Meredith joined them. "If I were you, I couldn't wait."

"If I were you, I would never let him go," Kate added with a sigh.

Fiona watched Ian as he pushed open the vestibule door. The falling snow tossed him in dark relief, and his silhouette made the real Ian much easier to see. They all thought Ian was a catch, but she knew the truth. There was true goodness in this world—goodness in the heart of the man who ambled out into the winter's cold. The door closed shut behind him and his image stayed with her, at the back of her mind and the core of her soul.

Chapter Fourteen

"Ooh, there *he* is, helping with the Christmas tree." Lila left no doubt as to who "he" was. "Ian is a nice man."

"Nice and good-looking. I approve." Meredith hooked her arm in Fiona's. The group was walking back from a meal at the boardinghouse owned by a church member who had spoiled them all with delicious roast beef sandwiches and chocolate cake. "I hate being away at school. I'm missing the good times and soon they will all be gone. First Fiona, and then one of you is next. By the time I come back in May, every one of you will be married."

"Fiona wouldn't get married so fast, would you, Fee?" Kate locked arms with her on the other side.

"What about finishing school?" Lila asked.

"I *will* be graduating." Thanks to Ian. If she walked on tiptoe she could see a glimpse of him, standing alongside Emmett Sims's teamster's sled, talking with a few other young men. None of them seemed as fine or as handsome as Ian McPherson. "He and I are not discussing weddings. We are strangers. I do not want to marry a stranger."

"Some people you meet right away and know better than someone you have known forever." Kate crinkled her brow thoughtfully. "True love might be like that. At least that's the way it is in all the stories. You find the right one for you, the other half of your soul. It's not about how much time you know someone."

"My parents were like that," Lila confessed, lowering her voice. Up ahead their nemesis, Narcissa Bell, was walking with her friends, within earshot. "They were school sweethearts. Ma said the first time she saw my pa, it was as if she had known him forever. One year later, they were married. They were happy."

"That's not a fairy tale, it's real," Kate said as if proof positive. "I have a feeling the same will happen to you, Fee. The way Ian has changed you—"

"I have *not* changed." Okay, maybe she said that a little too fast and with a telling ring of denial, but she was exactly the same girl she had been before Ian had rode into her life one snowy afternoon.

A note rang in her chest, an emotional pang that felt like the perfect chord played by both heart and soul. It came from simply remembering how he'd galloped after Flannigan with lasso circling, like a myth.

I'm starting to believe, she realized as the road brought her to the churchyard, where he stood talking to other young men near to his age. Every step brought her nearer, making it easy to see the details. The snow building on his hat brim, the dimples bracketing his cheeks, the lean line of his jaw, the laughter softening it.

She forgot that he was only a year older than her. Ian had become the head of his household when his grandfather passed away. He provided for his grandmother. Somehow he had managed his grandfather's debts and survived losing great wealth and valuable land, all with his dignity and spirit intact. He had not walked an easy road, and yet he'd done so without complaint or bitterness and with an injured leg.

Shame filled her because she had never asked him about it. She had wanted to keep distance between them; now, she no longer cared about that. She had been so concerned with what she wanted and couldn't have that she'd failed to see how he had tried to help her. He was having a hard time of it and she could have offered him an ear to listen and a friend to care.

He lit up when he saw her, and something within him was open, like a door letting in the light. He turned from his discussion with the Sims brothers and the reverend's son. Pure blue sparkles twinkled in his irises, like a rare jewel she had never seen before. There was much to admire about this man, more than she had let herself notice. Maybe—just maybe—she had noticed all along. She didn't want tender feelings for him taking root, but her will didn't seem to stop them. Affection for him kept struggling to life.

"I invited your fiancé to join us, Fiona," the reverend's son explained as he hefted the base of a cut fir tree from the teamster sled. "Something tells me you won't mind."

She blushed, feeling the weight of all eyes

turning to her. But it was Ian's silent question she noticed, the one that she heard without a single word. She did want him with her. She wanted him to have fun. "I was going to ask him to stay, too."

"Then grab a hand, McPherson." Austin Hadly was joined by the other young men in lifting the tree.

The fresh scent of evergreen sweetened the air, or maybe it was something else that made the afternoon perfect. She was hardly aware of other kids from her class clamoring up the street to help; Ian was all she could see. The ease as he grabbed the tree's trunk midway, his easy conversation with the other men, and the capable way he did everything. His baritone stood out from all the other voices in the yard, deep and rich and far too dear.

"Oh, you really do care about him." Kate squeezed her tightly.

"It's written all over your face." Meredith squeezed, too. "I'm happy for you, Fee."

"We all are," Scarlet added.

"But the real question is who will stand up for you at your wedding?" Lila's question, meant to tease, was a loving one.

"I do not know what I am going to do with the lot of you." Fiona rolled her eyes. "We should be thinking of decorating the tree and raising donations for the orphanage. Not thinking about something that will never happen. You all are putting the cart before the pony."

"Sure, but we keep hoping for you, Fee." Scarlet led the way to the front stairs.

"Hoping and praying," Kate added.

"Just because you have planned one future, doesn't mean something better can't happen." Meredith sounded as if she spoke from personal experience. "God might have other plans for you, Fee. Better ones."

"That's right. Maybe He is planning to give you a good family," Lila added as she followed Scarlet up the steps. "Maybe He wants you to have true love in your life, after all."

But I don't believe in true love. She bit her lip to hold back the words. The last thing she wanted to do was to spoil her friends' good cheer. Besides, they knew how she felt about placing her life in a man's hands. Even if they were Ian's. She slipped through the doorway toward him. He and Lorenzo were holding the tree upright while the reverend's son drove nails through the base and into the stand.

When his gaze met hers, she did not need words to know what he was thinking. She started to chuckle, just a little, and across the sanctuary he joined her. It felt as if their laughter lifted like prayers all the way to heaven.

He could have dreamed up the afternoon, drawing it with the soft slants of light through the windows—not harsh straight lines, but gentle, broken ones. The scene could have been something he had captured on paper, the regal tree and the hopeful young people surrounding it. The dance of lamplight on happy faces. Handmade and donated ornaments, some of fine crystal and porcelain, others of calico and lace, twirled on strings of red satin ribbon amid the dark stands of small white candles.

He moved the chair over a few feet and climbed back onto it. Through the boughs, he caught Lorenzo frowning at him. It took a bit to fight off another surge of jealousy. Those had been plaguing him all afternoon, ever since Fee stepped into church, snow dappled and luminous, more beautiful in her simple gingham dress and coat than he had ever seen her before. He feared he would never tire of seeing her; forever would be a long dark place when she was gone from his life. So he intended to cherish this time he had with her.

Judging by the adoration on the smitten Lorenzo's face, Ian was not alone in that wish.

"You have a good eye, McPherson," Austin Hadly commented from the next chair over. He finished twining a small candle holder to a sturdy bough and gave it a test to make sure it held tight. "Next year you should volunteer for the Christmas committee. We could use more men. I feel mighty outnumbered with all those matrons in the group."

"I suppose some of them will be by to inspect our work?"

"Without a doubt." Good-natured, the reverend's son chuckled, as if he enjoyed his work. "I saw that fine mare you were driving around town on Friday. I've never seen an animal like her."

"She is rare, my Duchess." He absently hung a porcelain angel on a branch. He heard Fiona's name murmured in the chorus of voices. His senses sharpened, aware when she spoke. In the dull roar of conversations, her alto was the one he heard above all the others.

"They did turn out very well this year." Fiona held up a snowflake, a fragile lacy concoction of thin white thread and air. He had hung ornaments just like the one she held up, one she had made, he realized. "I am finally getting the knack of tatting. Thanks to you, Scarlet."

"You are better at it than I ever was. I should have made snowflakes, too."

"I love your little embroidered manger scenes." Fiona, bent over her work on the front pew, tied a red ribbon into an ornament and fussed with the bow, tugging until it was perfect.

She made a picture with her china-doll face flushed pink and relaxed. Only the fading bruise of her black eye remained. He hated that she'd been hurt, but it would be the last time. He vowed it.

"Uh, Ian?"

He blinked. Austin was waiting, as if for an answer. Embarrassed to be caught watching the lass, with his feelings—he feared—revealed.

"The candles are up. Why don't you go fetch the last of the ornaments from the girls, and then we will all be done." Austin cleared his throat, probably trying not to laugh.

Sure, he felt like a sap as his feet hit the polished wood floor. The rest of the men gathered around the tree knew it, and he didn't miss the choked-back laughter as he walked away. Just wait, he wanted to tell them. Wait until a pretty lass comes along who turns your priorities upside down. Until there wasn't anything a man wouldn't give to make her life better.

"Are you glad you stayed to help?" Fiona asked, unaware of how vulnerable she made him with that curve of her smile and her sweet spirit.

"Aye. I haven't had this much fun since I was in school." Before Grandfather's illness had taken him out of the classroom for good. Life had been far too serious.

"You have made friends." She looked pleased, as if that was her hope. "I mean, if you are going to be staying here, it might be nice for you to know people. So you aren't so alone."

His throat closed, and he could not speak. Ah, but her caring touched him and made the losses in his life smaller and the hardships easier.

"That is the last of them." One of the girls—the red-haired one—shoved the box into his hand. He suspected Fiona's friends saw right through him to his eternal devotion. To his enduring, lifelong love.

A love that likely would never be returned.

He clutched the box, realizing he still could not speak. He feared Fiona, too, could see far too much. It was for her that he gave a shrug, as if to make up for his silence, and turned away.

"I will take those." Lorenzo took the ornaments, his manner gruff, although Ian sensed he did not mean to be.

He knew how it felt not to have affection for Fiona returned. He felt an odd empathy with the young man as they stood side by side, hanging the last of the decorations in the uppermost branches.

The chairs were pulled away and all in the room gathered close to admire the tree. Everything passed in a haze for him: the cacophony of movement and noise, the joyful discussions, the call to join hands in prayer. Fiona slipped into line beside him, her soft hand finding his. That surprised him, as did her tight grip. All through the prayer, he did his best to keep from asking the Lord above for what he wanted most. As the group prayed for compassion and peace and for the welfare of others, he did, too.

He prayed for Fiona. Not that he would win her love, but that she would have her heart's desire. Beyond all that he wished for himself, none of it mattered a bit in comparison with all he wanted for her.

Coziness clung to her and chased away the shocking cold as they sped toward home. The town was a shadow in the falling twilight behind them, and the road ahead ribboned across the gently rolling prairie. Tonight the wind did not whisper to her as she drew the blanket up to her chin. Whatever the world held out there could not be as rosy as what Ian had given her here.

"Do you think you will like staying in Angel Falls?" She felt shy, her voice strangely thin, but she attributed it to the bitter temperatures.

"I like it just fine. This place will be a new start for me, different from all that I knew. Maybe I can find my future here in this land of wide-open prairie and of mountains that hold up the sky."

"Spoken like a man who is thinking of drawing those mountains."

"How did you know?"

"You are less and less a stranger to me."

"I feel as if you never were, lass."

It was pure kindness, plain and simple, a sign of his compassionate nature, that was all. Fiona fisted her hands inside her mittens, determined to be practical and sensible.

"What kind of start did you have in mind?" Snowflakes sifted through the air between them, perhaps hiding what she really wanted to know. "Will you move north if you get a job at the mill?"

"I need wages, lass, but I can ride the five-mile stretch and live here."

Why could she see the colors of his dreams? Green like the fields in May, sapphire-blue like the Montana summer sky and dotted with horses of every color, their velvet coats gleaming in the sun. "You will work to buy horses again. To build another stable."

"Once, we had more than two hundred horses grazing on our land. More than a few of them were champions. Now, the twelve are all I have left."

She felt his loss, not for the former prestige of his family but for the horses he had loved. "You helped to raise and train them, didn't you?"

"The hardest losses are of the heart, it's true." His throat worked, and his jaw turned to iron. "The horses I have left were the ones I could not part with."

"Where are they now?"

"A neighbor is boarding them for me. He's a good friend, and he bought all of my family's land. It is his house where my grandmother is staying."

"Have you heard from her?"

"No, but I expect a letter in the mail any day. This is the first Christmas we will spend apart."

"What was Christmas like for your family?"

"Nana would always serve a roasted duck, candied yams and her mother's baked bean recipe. Buttermilk biscuits light enough to float in midair. Hot chocolate and angel food cake afterward by the fire. That was Christmas dinner."

"You mean there is more?"

"Presents piled under the tree. Christmas Eve service the night before, of course. We would have dinner in town at the hotel after a day of stringing popcorn and making cookies. When I was a little tyke, I would help my mother decorate the Christmas cookies. After she passed, Nana and I carried on the tradition. Nana would spend part of both days playing Christmas carols on her piano. We would gather round with eggnog or tea and sing until we were hoarse."

"You have lived a dream, Ian. Or at least, a dream to some people."

"I'll not argue." The rundown shanty where Fiona's friend lived came into sight, the few windows glowing across the ever darkening landscape. He gave Flannigan more rein, letting the horse run some, as he seemed to want to do.

"One day I pray you have that again." Her hand covered his, and through the layers of wool and leather, he could feel the depth of her wish for him.

The heavens were kind to him and saved him from answering, for the driveway rolled into sight and beyond that the joyless shanty with one window aglow with light.

"We're home." She breathed the words out like a sigh, and it was as if the twilight fell with her happiness.

"I pray that one day home will be a welcome place for you, pretty girl." He reined the horse toward the barn, drawing him gently in from his run. Because he did not want to reveal anything more, he let silence settle between them. Her hand remained on his until the sled came to a stop.

"Next time, Fee, be kinder to the poor young men who have lost their hearts to you." He dragged away from her side, hating to put distance between them.

"What are you talking about?" She scowled, her face scrunching up adorably.

Sad that he was falling ever harder for her. Love was not finite, he realized. It was an infinite place that kept pulling a man apart. Resigned, he offered to help her from the sled, but she hopped out on the other side.

"Lorenzo." He patted Flannigan before kneeling to unbuckle the harnessing. "And those other school boys. What were their names? James and Luken and that blond-headed kid."

"Funny. What could have possibly given you the idea that half the graduating class of boys is carrying a torch for me? Surely." She rolled her eyes, laughing at him, unaware of the doting man who stood right in front of her. Of course she had not noticed the others, either.

"I am telling you the truth." He worked one buckle free and circled around for another. "You are breaking hearts, Fiona, right and left. Think of the poor fellows, would you? It is all I am asking."

"No one is ever going to love me." She looked vulnerable in the thickening twilight, certain as she tucked her Bible into the crook of her arm. "I don't intend to let anyone close enough to try."

"What? Not even me?" Instead of working the harness free, he ambled closer. "I heard you and your girlfriends. It sounds like you've already let me far too close."

"*They* were talking about weddings and forever, not me." Her voice trembled. "I hope you don't think I told them—"

"No," he interrupted, saving her from having to say the words aloud. "We both agreed there would be no wedding. Just a long engagement."

"Yes." She didn't move away. She didn't look away. She couldn't. "I hope this will be a benefit for you, too. I hate to think that your staying here for me would hinder your dreams."

"I am exactly where I want to be. Trust that." His knuckles grazed her cheek tenderly. "You are wrong about my dreams, Fiona. The only ones I have are for you."

Chapter Fifteen

What was the man doing to her? He made it impossible to forget him. All night long he had snuck into her dreams like a bandit, out to steal her heart. *I could not make myself ride another step east, so I followed my heart back to you. I'm going to make sure you are never frightened like that again.*

All morning his velvet-coated promises and declarations drove out all other thoughts. Standing at the front of the classroom, she gripped her hands, trying in vain to find historical facts in her head. But all she could locate were Ian's startling confessions. *You are wrong about my dreams, Fiona. The only ones I have are for you.*

What did that mean? Surely she was not part of his dreams. No, that could not be right.

He had meant that he wanted her happiness. As a friend might.

A friend. That's what she was to him. That was exactly what she wanted to be. And if disappointment whispered through her, she was determined to ignore it.

"Miss O'Rourke," the teacher scolded, her frown as severe as her tone. "I'm afraid you will have to study this lesson again."

"I'm sorry, Miss Lambert." Miserable, she hung her head. She could not remember what she had learned about the battle of Gettysburg. There was nothing in her mind but Ian.

Lila grabbed hold of her hand and squeezed in sympathy.

"That is all, class. You may return to your seats." Miss Lambert laid her history book on her desk, watchful as the twelfth-grade students filed down the aisles, quietly so as not to disturb the others who were studying industriously.

Fiona slipped into her desk. She had never failed a lesson before. She wanted to blame Ian, but the fault was hers. She was the one who could not stop the images of him in the barn doing the evening chores, of how relaxed the horses and the cow were in his presence and how happy they seemed. She hardly recognized Flannigan, who no longer looked prairie-ward with longing in his eyes. Ian, who had walked her to the house and with one stare at her da, ensured that not one cruel word was spoken to her. Ian, who had driven her to school in the morning, helping her from the sled at the schoolyard, tipping his hat in goodbye to her like any courting man.

He was being polite, that was all. No need to read anything more into it. She stacked her books, hearing the school bell ring. Noise burst out around her. Books slammed shut, kids bounced up from their seats, shoes knelled against the floorboards. Conversations drowned out the last echoes of the bell. All she could think about was seeing Ian again. Knowing he would be waiting for her outside Miss Sims's shop was like a gift, one she couldn't wait for.

"Poor Lorenzo hasn't been the same since he met Ian." Scarlet leaned close, whispering as they made their way through the emptying classroom. "I think you broke his heart, Fee."

"Whose heart?" She wondered if Ian would be shivering in his too-thin coat.

"I think she did, too." Lila spoke up, all sympathy. "Maybe I can offer him a few kind words during caroling practice to soothe his wounded feelings."

"You certainly should." Earlee's wistfulness was that of a staunch romantic. "Lorenzo does look downcast today, poor dear."

"And it's all Fee's fault." Kate winked.

"What did I do?" she asked, hardly realizing she hadn't buttoned her coat yet. In fact, she couldn't remember fetching her coat from the hallway or walking through the schoolroom, or even getting up from her desk. The sunshine blinded her as she waltzed out into the winter afternoon, squinting against the brightness as she searched the roadway for him. Ridiculous, because she knew he wouldn't be there, but did that stop her from looking for him? Not one bit.

"There's no sense trying to talk to her," Scarlet said, chuckling warmly. "I talked Ma into making a cake for our party on Friday."

"Perfect. My stepmother is going to help me fix chicken and dumplings." Lila sounded excited. "Fiona, will you bring the biscuits?"

"Sure." She didn't realize how much she could miss Ian. It made no sense. It wasn't as if she cared for the man, right?

"My brother has agreed to come fetch me

if the weather is bad, so I can come for sure," Kate commented happily.

"That's wonderful!" Earlee clasped her hands together prayerfully. "This might be our last celebration together. Our sewing circle might break apart after graduation. You never know where life will take each one of us."

"I hadn't thought of it that way." Fiona sank into the snow, but it was more than her shoe sliding into the icy drift. "Our last sewing-circle Christmas party. That sounds so sad."

"Depressing," Scarlet agreed. "Which is why we do not have to think about it. Instead, it will be the best party we have ever had."

They parted ways—Scarlet and Lila headed off to the church for caroling practice, Kate climbed into her father's sleigh and Earlee walked away with six of her younger siblings. She did not have time to walk uptown today, for she was needed at home.

It was a beautiful day. The sun tossed diamonds onto the pristine snow, and she followed its sparkling trail. She was as cheerful as the lemony rays of sunshine, thinking of the tatted snowflakes she had finished and blued last night. They would be dry and perfect when she got home. Her gifts for her friends were done. Her parents did not celebrate Christmas with gifts, so she had all the presents she would need for the holiday—all but one.

Ian. Her thoughts looped back to him. All roads led inexorably to him. The church steeple rose above the cluster of trees and the tall storefronts, reminded her of how perfect yesterday after the church service had been. The looks they had shared across the sanctuary, how Ian had appeared different with worries and responsibilities lifted from his strapping shoulders. Of what he had told her about his family and his grandmother. She thought of the older woman, who had been best friends with her grandmother.

In her mind's eye she could see her own grandmother's kind face as she told of the McPhersons. Love, she realized, was the reason Ian was here—for his grandmother, and respect for what two girlfriends had shared long ago.

She turned onto the main street, snow tumbling off her shoes and onto the boardwalk. Perhaps, then, it was not so strange she and Ian felt such strong friendship for one another. Maybe she did not need to fight it so much.

"Good afternoon, Fiona," Cora Sims greeted from behind the front desk. "It has been a busy day. Let me finish up this sale, and I will be right with you. There is tea steeping on the stovetop. It will warm you right up."

"Thank you, Miss Sims." Fiona liked the older woman. Cora Sims had been her inspiration for her future life. The lady had come to town long ago and started her own dress shop. She had made a fine life for herself, sewing for others. Maybe, thanks to Ian's help, she could do the same one day.

What used to give her joy to think about now weighed her down. That future did not seem as bright. It was not only the prospect of leaving her friends, but something else. Something that hurt worse, and that made no sense.

Ian. She felt his presence as surely as the warmth from the stove. She unbuttoned her coat, searching for him through the wide display window. There he was across the street, confident and manly, tethering Flannigan to the hitching post. The big horse nudged the man's hand affectionately, as if wanting one last nose rub. Ian obviously agreed, his affection clear. He was a true horseman in a worn-thin coat. He had to be freezing, his teeth looked to be chattering, but he made no hurry to end his time with Flannigan to rush out of the cold.

"I'm pleased to see you, Fiona. I hope this means you have the basting done so soon?"

"Yes, Miss Sims. I worked most of the weekend on it." She opened her book bag and carefully withdrew the folded dress. "The collar was tricky, but I got it set just right. See what you think."

While the seamstress shook out the garment to study it, Fiona let her attention wander back to the street. Ian had left Flannigan's side and was lumbering up the steps onto the boardwalk, cane in hand. The sun brightened because he was near. Tenderness stirred within her, reverent and sweet. Tenderness she wanted to deny, but couldn't.

"This is excellent work, Fiona. Let me get your wages."

She blinked; for a second she had forgotten where she was. She nervously brushed a curl behind her ear. "Do you have any good heavy wool in stock? Something suitable for a winter coat?"

"Some new bolts came in on Friday's train." Cora tapped toward the front desk. "I put them out this morning. Just to your left, next to the buttons display."

It did not make any sense to spend so much money, but did that stop her from wandering over to the table? Not one bit. There was no looking or debating. A bolt of black wool stood out from all the others, and she snatched it without thought. The finest quality, judging from its weight. She didn't even ask Cora the price per yard.

"Will you hold this for me?" she asked. "I can come by after school tomorrow to pay for it."

"That would be fine." Cora smiled knowingly as she took the quality fabric and unrolled it with a thump onto the cutting counter. "Why don't I cut it for you now, and you can take it with you? That way you can get started on it tonight. Christmas is fast approaching. How many yards do you need?"

"Enough for a man's coat," she whispered, for the bell above the door jingled. Ian's uneven step tapped into the store, the sound meaningful to her. This was more than friendship she felt. Much more. Ignoring it or denying it would not change that fact.

"I've had a talk with your horse." He took off his hat, revealing a relaxed, happy smile.

He must have gotten the job. "Flannigan would like you to drive him home."

"How thoughtful of him." She stepped away from the counter, hoping Ian would not notice the fabric. "What else did Flannigan say?"

"That he misses you. You used to spend your evenings in the barn."

"And he would like me to do that again, would he?"

"I believe so. I'm sure Riley would not mind at all, either." He held out his hands to warm them at the stove. "Or the cat. He has set his cap for you, I fear."

"Oh, you do not fool me one bit, McPherson."

"McPherson, is it? Again? You must be mad at me."

"Blaming all that on the animals. Yes, indeed. If you want me to know you wouldn't mind sharing the barn with me in the evening, then you could simply say so." She thanked the shop owner with a conspiratorial smile and tucked a brown-wrapped package into her book bag. "Thank you, Miss Sims. Have a good afternoon!"

"Goodbye, dear. Same to you." The sewing lady looked mighty pleased and gave him an approving smile. He had been getting a lot of those lately. Word had traveled about town he was here to marry the O'Rourke girl. Her hardships were no secret, nor could they be with the fading yellow bruise on her cheek-bone.

Gentleness filled him. He resisted the need to pull her close and lay an arm around her shoulder. He wanted her step to remain light as she waltzed to the door. He opened it for her and followed her into the sunshine gracing the boardwalk.

"Did you get work?" She whirled around in a swirl of red gingham. "You look happy, so that must mean yes."

"Aye. I start in the morning. I'm afraid you will have to walk to school."

"I don't mind. I usually stop by Earlee's house so I can walk most of the way with her." She skipped down the steps, her twin braids flying behind her.

He would forever remember this picture of her with dark wisps curling around her heart-shaped face, her happiness contagious, her wholesome beauty.

"C'mon, Ian. I can't wait to drive." She glided across the street, one step ahead and all that was dear to him. Her dark hair gleamed blue-black, her porcelain skin blushed by the winter air.

How precious this time with her was, he realized as he followed her across the road. The bustle of town, the approaching whistle of the train, the too-slow beat of his pulse were too commonplace for this moment. When Fiona turned to him, he sensed more than tolerance in her manner. Perhaps more than friendship.

"I see you have had a very busy day without me." She touched his sleeve, nodding toward the sled's bed. "What do you have under the tarp?"

"Fence posts. When I went to repair the broken board in the corral, I decided it would do little good if the post was ready to fall down. So I stopped by the lumberyard."

"I'm sure Flannigan will be pleased. He will get to romp in the corral again. Right, boy?" Although she had drifted away from his side, a form of closeness remained. A tie Ian could not explain or prove, but he felt it.

Or he surely hoped he did. He worked the tether free, watching as Fiona ran her fingers through the horse's forelock. He enjoyed her musical laugh as the gelding tossed his head, preferring to have his nose stroked instead.

"All right, have your way, big fella." She

obliged. "As long as you know I am boss when we drive home."

The gelding nickered low in his throat, perhaps a bit of a protest, and Ian felt hope as Fiona laughed again. She had the kind of spirit that she would be happy wherever her future took her.

"Did you hear that, Ian? I think he is planning on giving me some trouble." She didn't look worried, no, she looked like perfection. She was his dream come true.

Please, Lord, he prayed. *If it is Your will, let her know it one day. I am a patient man. I do not mind waiting.*

No answer came from above, but then, he did not expect one so soon. He took hold of the driving reins, for the gelding did have trouble glinting in his adoring eyes. He knew just how the horse felt.

"Aye, I think Flannigan is making plans." He helped her into the sled, something he wouldn't mind doing the rest of his life. "I guess you had best be making some plans of your own."

"You're going to leave me to deal with him if he runs away?"

"Don't think you can give over the reins to me when times get tough." He spread the lap blanket over her, tucking it in so she would be warm.

"Who else would I turn to, Ian?" She took the reins from him, but it felt as if she took something else. Likely it was his eternal devotion, for she already had his love. "There is no one else in this sled."

"You think I will rescue you whenever you need it, is that it?" He settled on the seat beside her, taking care to double the blanket over so that she had all of it. The thermometer in the tailor's store window said it was fifteen degrees below. "You know me too well, for I will always be here when you need me."

"I know." Deeper meaning layered her words and chased away every shadow. What she didn't say—perhaps what she couldn't—remained between them, a sweetness he felt soul deep.

"I care for you, too, lass." He tried to keep all the affection he felt from his voice, but he failed. It was too great to hide, too powerful to hold back. Like an avalanche it crashed through him.

Never in his life had there been a love like this. He laid an arm across the back of the seat and drew Fiona close against him. She did not shy away. She bowed her head, studying the reins for a moment as if she could find some answer there.

Flannigan broke the moment and darted into the street before Ian could know Fiona's reaction. Would she say the same, or would she turn away from him? The horse had impeccable timing, that was for sure.

"Tighten the reins more," he advised. "A little heavier bit will give you more control."

"I like going fast." She didn't draw up the reins but she didn't move away, either. The town's last block flew by in a blur and they raced toward the dazzling white prairie together, blessed by a winter-blue sky.

Storm clouds gathered at the horizon, but for this perfect moment it was a clear day.

Fiona loved driving. She loved the feel of Flannigan's strength telegraphing down the thick leather reins and into her hands. She liked being the one to direct the horse, to give him his head so he could run as fast as he wanted and she would feel the wind whipping through her hair.

"You are as bad as the gelding." Ian's hands closed over hers. "You will have to slow him down or we will never make the turn."

"You're afraid I am going to crash your

sled." She rather liked that his arms were around her, and she leaned into the curve of his chest. Never had she felt so safe and comforted. Nothing in her life had ever been like this. She was utterly secure and gently cherished.

This cannot be love, she told herself firmly. Sure, it was a great deal more than friendship, but she wasn't the kind of girl who lost her heart.

"I'm afraid you are going to tumble us into the ditch." He was laughing. "While you probably think that is nothing less than I deserve, that's how I broke my leg in the first place."

"In a sleigh accident?"

"No, going too fast. In a race." He tensed, every muscle, every tendon. Tightness snapped in his jaw. "You haven't been so wrong about me. I was once a desperate man."

It was hard to believe he would do something wrong. "What happened?"

"After selling off parcels of our land, I couldn't stand to do the same with our last quarter-section. Raising and training horses is an expensive endeavor, especially when a false rumor made my last customers panic. Owners pulled their thoroughbreds from my training stable, and I was left with bills I couldn't pay. That had been my hope to restore the family name—training winners for other men so I could bankroll the training of our champions."

"It was a gamble." She saw the cost. The wince of pain, and the weight of his failure. "You lost because of someone's cruel words about you?"

"Worse than that, afterward I took a bet. I know the Lord frowns on such things, but I didn't want to have to explain to my grandmother she would have to leave her home. The house Grandfather had built for her was filled with all the memories of their life together. So I bet the rest of my land, and all but a dozen horses, that I could win a cross-country race. Not a legal race, mind you, on the track. But a private one through the low country, dangerous to man and beast. It was funded by wealthy men. The chance to win so much money was something I could not turn down."

"You would have lost your family home anyway."

"That was my reasoning. My justification to do what I knew was wrong. But the lure of winning a fine amount of money was enough to make me saddle my best stallion and ride."

"And you fell?"

"The horse landed wrong on a jump over a fallen tree. He broke two legs and had to be put down. The cost of my foolishness." He pulled away, withdrawing his arm from her shoulders. Maybe it was because the sled had come to a stop. He studied the horizon, where the first blaze of sunset stained the encroaching clouds. "I splinted my leg, carved a pair of crutches and pressured men I knew for a job. I cleaned stalls day and night."

"On an injured leg?"

"I could not lie abed. Nana was ill, there were enough doctor bills without my adding to them. So I did what I had to do. I kept a roof over my grandmother's head and her needs met." He cleared his throat, battling something she could not see.

Flannigan nickered, tossing his head for attention, reminding her she held the reins still. They had reached the barn, she realized, but she could not move. Ian felt distant, as if he were miles away instead of beside her. She wanted to reach out to him, but she stayed motionless on the seat. "A lot of men would not have stayed in the first place. They would have fled their responsibilities."

He said nothing more, although his throat worked, as if he had more to say. He swept off his hat, knocking snow from the brim, but he could not hide his trembling. From cold, from the failure dogging him, perhaps from something more she could not see.

"Come on." He climbed out of the sled. "Flannigan isn't happy standing. It's too cold, and he's worked up a lather."

Fiona wasn't fooled. Whatever Ian's faults and the mistakes he had made, he had done them for the greatest reason of all—love. Respect filled her, slow and sweet and endlessly deep.

He lifted the blanket away from her and folded it so that she would not trip on its cumbersome length. When he gave her his hand, as he always did, as she knew he always would, a force swept through her. She loved him. She wished she could stop it, hold back her tenderness like a dam in high water, but she could not.

Chapter Sixteen

"Fiona! You daft girl! You are spilling water all over the floor."

Ma's shrill tone, full of fury, penetrated Fiona's thoughts. She realized she was kneeling on the kitchen floor, her hands wrist deep in suds. The edge of the washboard dug into her ribs.

"Staring off into nothing when you should be finishing the wash. You're lazier than ever, girl." Footsteps pounded from the table to the stove, and sizzling erupted when the cut potatoes hit the hot fry pan. "I do not approve of that man."

"I rather like him." She gripped a pair of her father's trousers in both hands and scoured them on the washboard.

"You say that now." Ma turned, spatula in

hand. "Do not think you are so smart, missy. That is the way men are, pretending to be kind and good to you when they want something. Aye, they can sweet-talk you into believing they would do anything for you. All that matters is your happiness. Sound familiar?"

How did her mother know? Her strength faltered, the garment caught midstroke, and she skinned her knuckles on the corrugated washboard. A streak of blood stained her raw skin. "You and Da have been listening in—"

"Uh! As if I need to." Ma's laugh rang high and cruel. "I have walked in your shoes before. How else do you think I married your da?"

"I—" The garment in the tub was blurry, probably due to the effects of the soapy water.

"I was sixteen, and the man who came courting, the man my parents picked for me, was charming. Bringing me flowers and notions for my sewing. I was making a wedding ring quilt for my hope chest." Ma left the pan sizzling, pounding closer. "Oh, I fell heart and soul for the man who treated me like such a lady, who held doors for me and pledged his undying affection. Who wanted me to have all of my dreams."

Fiona wished the barbed words did not find their target, but they did. She kept wringing, and over the splash of the rinse water she heard the echo of Ian's promises. *I followed my heart back to you. The only dreams I have are for you. I care for you, lass.*

He had told her the truth. She would have known if he had been false. She plopped the trousers into the clothes basket and reached for a nearby towel. She would not listen to her mother: it was simply years of unhappiness that made her say terrible things.

"Don't believe me." Ma returned to the stove, stirring the potatoes harder than necessary. Several flew out of the pan and she left them to smoke. "You think your charming Mr. McPherson is a shining knight now, but mark my words. He is out for himself, as all men are."

Don't listen to her, Fee. She mopped up the last of the splashed water and scooped the clothes basket off the floor. Her parents were unhappy with the way Ian was changing things. Da was unhappy that he was no longer in complete control. That was all this was. Her mother's hurtful words could not be true. She unhooked her coat from the peg and slipped into it.

"Don't have anything to say, girl? I know what you are thinking. You think your man is nothing like your da. That's what I thought about *your* father, that he was not like mine." Ma shook her head, grown too hard with her disappointments in life to care about the hurt she was causing. "You might as well smarten up, girl. We are wasting time waiting for the wedding. Marry the boy. I am on pins and needles not knowing for sure if he will keep his word."

"I have never said I would marry Ian, and besides, he has paid the bank." All the proof she needed that her mother was not right. She grabbed the latch and tugged. The door squeaked open.

"No, he has not. He has only promised to. He went and got some fancy lawyer involved."

"Whatever Ian is doing, he is a fair man." She did not need to list all that he had done for her to prove it. It was one of the things she admired about him. Besides, he had said he didn't want the farm because of the high mortgage, the very reason Da could not easily sell it. "You shouldn't worry so, Ma."

"No man is fair. Can't you get that through your thick head? Forget this foolishness. Let us get on to the business of saving our home. I am not going to live out of the back of our wagon."

This was what twenty years of unhappiness and unkindness could do to a person, eroding away the tender places. She could not listen to any more; she wrestled down anger as she drew the door closed.

Ma's final words drifted out to her. "The moment he gets his name on the deed, he will change, and not for the better. All he wants is the land. So stop being difficult and marry him now—"

The door clicked shut and Fiona walked away with a heavy heart. Glad she was that Ian wanted her to spend the evenings with him in the barn. She might not be able to work on his coat, but she could make a pattern for it. Perhaps get measurements from his clothes, if she offered to wash them. Her step quickened as she hurried down the steps and plunged into the snowy path.

The glow from the faded sunset blessed the silent prairie with a rare light. She walked on lavender-hued snow toward the clothesline, breathing in the wonder of the prairie. The hush felt reverent, almost sacred, almost as if God was peering down from heaven through the ragged clouds. One star twinkled at the horizon's edge, a reminder that night was coming.

What was Ian doing? She caught sight of the sled, drawn up to the corral's gate. Perhaps he was inside taking care of Flannigan. She let the basket drop to the ground and dug a half-dozen wooden pins from the hanging bag. She clipped them to the top of her apron before shaking the wrinkles from the first garment she grabbed. Thinking of him made her worries lighter. She did not fret over Ma's words, because she trusted Ian. The safety and comfort she'd felt in his arms remained like a gift, one she had never guessed could be so wonderful.

She clipped up one pair of Da's trousers, and reached for another pair. The wind stirred around her in little swirls, and snowflakes lifted from the ground in a slow, circling waltz. It did feel as if heaven were nearer, she thought, as she reached for another garment to hang.

A rumbling disrupted the prairie's peace, angry tones skimming the darkening snow as if riding the wind. They came too softly at first to hear more than the rise and fall of baritone and tenor, but as she reached for another clothespin, the wind shifted to bring the words straight to her.

"—that is one point I won't budge on, O'Rourke. Fiona is—"

"—my daughter, and she stays and takes care of us. We are not as young as we used to be. That's the deal."

"No, that's not the deal I shook on."

"It is if you want the deed signed over to you. Isn't that what you want? Isn't the land the reason you are here?"

"Aye."

The clothespins slipped from her fingers and plinked to the ground. Night fell like a blanket over the land and over her shock.

She could not be hearing them right. There had to be a rational explanation.

"Good. I've spoken with the sheriff. He will be performing the ceremony at noon the day after Christmas. Agreed?"

The wind gusted, stealing Ian's answer. It didn't matter. She didn't need to hear him agree. She hadn't misunderstood. She had heard him loud and clear.

Isn't the land the reason you are here?

Aye. He'd answered with resignation, but he had answered with the truth. His first priority was the land—not her. It always had been.

She had been too blind to see it. He had lied to her, and she had believed it.

She had loved him for it.

The first crack of pain struck like a blow. She grasped at the fallen pins, her fingers fumbling, her whole heart shattering one tiny piece at a time. The snow swirled whimsically at her feet, as if all were right with the world. Stars popped out like hope renewed, as she turned her back on the barn and the men there.

Maybe if she held herself very still inside the pain would stop. She managed to gather the last fallen clothespin and stood, feeling dizzy. The terrible truth would twirl away like a thousand crystal snowflakes and would be lost on the lonesome prairie. She could go back to believing in the cocoon of Ian's safe comfort and the hopeful love she felt for him.

A love he did not harbor for her. By rote, she grabbed another piece of laundry from the basket. The second crack of pain hit her like the strap cutting deep. For Ian, she was a means to an end, that was all. Just like her mother had said.

"Fiona! What are you doing, standing around like a loon? Get finished up there."

Ma marched into sight. "I need help with supper."

"Yes, Ma." She clipped the last garment—Ma's Sunday dress—to the line. The cold did not touch her as she grabbed the empty basket and tromped toward the house. The darkness trailed her through the deep drifts, past the strap on the lean-to wall and into the house where more work waited.

I don't like the way you are doin' things. O'Rourke's words taunted him as he beat the ground with the ax. Chunks of frozen soil and sod spewed into the night. Sweat rolled down his face as he swung again. The leverage he had on the man was gone; the tables had turned. Nana had somehow found the money to pay the man his asking price. *Fiona is mine, and until you put a ring on her finger, you will not be letting her drive a horse or go running off with those snooty friends of hers.*

Oh, but he was in a temper. He drove the ax downward a final time. Flannigan's nicker reminded him he was not alone in the corral. He leaned on the ax handle, pulled a handkerchief out of his back denims pocket and swiped the sweat off his face. His breath rose like smoke in the dark. Overhead all but a few stars kept watch; a storm was moving in.

"Sorry, boy. Let me chain up one last post and after we get it moved, I will treat you to a nice long—" A shadow moved at the edge of his vision, a slim, willowy form in a familiar gray coat. "Fiona. It is too cold for you to be out."

"Oh, and it's not for you?" Her chin went up, the faint starlight finding her.

"Point taken." He leaned the ax handle against the pile of rotting posts he'd extracted. "Is that supper I smell?"

"Yes. When you didn't come in to eat, I set a plate aside for you." She stopped to pat Flannigan, and probably to feed him a treat, as the horse lapped her palm and crunched away. Sounded like a carrot.

"You are an industrious man. Some would wait until morning to start refencing." She held out a cloth-covered plate. "Smarter men might wait for spring."

"I never claimed to be a smart man." He took it, aware that while she was only a few steps from him, she felt a mile away. The plate's heat penetrated his leather gloves, proof she had taken care to heat the food well for the trip outside. Thoughtful she was; his chest felt wrenched apart.

If you want the land in your name, you will marry her. O'Rourke's demands rocked through him. He set the plate on the flat-topped fence post before he dropped it. *I'm back in charge now. I have your grandmother's money, and I am through waiting. That girl is a burden, and you will take over the cost of supporting her or find another ranch.*

With his financial position, no bank would give him a mortgage. Ian's stomach soured, hating his choices. "I start my job in the morning, so if I want to get this repaired, then I have to work in the evenings."

"Repairing? No, that's replacing a board or two. You are putting in a whole new fence." She crossed her arms over her midsection, and with the wind whipping at her skirts, she looked oddly alone and lost. "Are you bringing your horses out here from Kentucky, then?"

"Aye. I can sell one of them to pay for the rail costs. But I would rather wait to see how much of my wages I can save and pay for it that way." His hand trembled as he tried to hold the plate steady and lifted the cloth. The buttery scent of hot biscuits and the meaty fried salt pork made his stomach growl, although he did not feel hungry. He was speaking of his dreams, when he had promised to protect hers. "In truth, I don't know how it is going to work out."

"That is the problem with the future. You cannot see it ahead of time." There was no greater beauty than Fiona in the stardust. Wherever she moved, the light hurried as if to illuminate her path. She climbed onto the remaining part of the fence and swung over to sit on the top rail, and the starlight lovingly pearled her hair and kissed her dear face.

Love for her filled every crack and hollow in him. He wished that an answering love would show on her face. Impossible, he knew, but maybe with time she would do more than care for him. Looked like now that time had run out, it was not to be.

He hardly tasted the biscuit or the butter melting on his tongue. How did he tell her what his grandmother had done? He took another bite, memorizing the way she balanced like a lost princess on the barnyard fence. She perched, straight-backed and regal, a spirit of dignity and composure in gingham and braids.

"Will you be bringing out your grandmother, too? You must worry about her." Her question came gently, laced with understanding.

"Aye. I'm guilty for leaving her. If I bring her here, I fear she will be disappointed in the prospects." He cut into the slice of salt pork with his fork. "She was expecting a grand place."

"Tell me about her."

"She is absolute kindness. I cannot remember her ever speaking a harsh word." He missed Nana, but all things changed. He was no longer a boy riding home from school at a racing gallop to tell her of his perfect marks for the day and to share cookies and milk on the front veranda. "She managed all my childhood mistakes with patience. She comforted my grandfather when my father's gambling ways had shamed them and later when his investments went bust. When I lost what was left, she did not once think of herself. Her only concern was for me. Misplaced, aye, and what I did not deserve."

"You must love her beyond measure."

"She is in large part to blame for the man I am."

"So I see." Flannigan wandered over, nosing for more treats. She pulled a carrot from her coat pocket and broke it in half. The crack resounded in the forlorn yard, as if emphasizing the broken-down poverty of the place.

The wind stirred the tendrils that had escaped from her braids as she leaned her forehead against the horse's neck. He wished he knew what would become of them all—a used-up horseman, an old gelding and a Cinderella girl with no prince to save her.

"You should bring her here." She broke the silence between them. "You worry about her disappointment, but from what you have told me, she could never be disappointed in you. She loves you, and she is family. That is what matters."

"True." He wondered at the sorrow on her face, but there was no hint of it in her voice or in the way she dropped from the fence post with a hop. Her skirts swirled around her and her braids thumped against her back. He resisted the urge to draw her into his arms and hold her close, to keep her safe and snug against his chest.

Instead he watched her take the empty plate and utensils, the cloth and his dreams.

"Good night," she said, but it felt like goodbye.

She took the starlight with her. The night

deepened, the shadows took over and the first flakes of snow tumbled from an unforgiving sky. A blast of brutal wind razored through his coat as if it were nothing; he was glad when the flash of light of a door opening told him Fiona had reached the warmth of the shanty.

The snowfall tumbled like a blanket from heaven, stealing away all sight of her.

She wrung the last drops of water from the fine wool fabric. The splashes and plunks of the droplets made a pleasant melody as she worked. She could not return cut fabric, and she didn't want to. There was nothing to be done but to continue on with the coat. The storm gusted against the eaves, echoing in the rafters inches above her head. Her attic bedroom might be small, but the heat radiating off the chimney stones kept her warm enough. But what of Ian? Was he still out there struggling to rebuild what he had lost?

She wanted to hate him for his deception, for the omission he had kept from her about buying the land anyway. She wanted a great many things as she hung the thick wool over a makeshift line. The fabric would be dry by morning and tomorrow she would work out a pattern for it. Maybe when she stopped by Miss Sims's store, she could ask the seamstress's advice.

You are a fool of the first water, Fiona O'Rourke. She wiped her damp hands on her apron. She had only herself to blame if her heart was broken. She had started to believe in stories and in schoolgirl fancies that had no place in a life like hers. She was not Meredith from a fine family or Lila with dreams to spare. She did not have Kate's optimism or Scarlet's indomitable ways. Stories did not fill her heart like they did Earlee's. She did not believe in storing away treasures in a hope chest or placing her trust in a man's love.

But hadn't she done that anyway—just a bit—without noticing it? She hefted the small buckets of rinse water and suds and carried them down the ladder. The splash of water and clink of the metal emphasized the emptiness of the kitchen, the barrenness of the home.

As she padded by the doorway, she caught sight of Da asleep in his chair. The empty bottle of whiskey reflected the single lamp's glow. Ma's rocking chair was empty. It was late; likely she had gone off to bed, but her hard words about men came alive in the kitchen again. Try as she might, she could not silence them. The memory kept rolling through her as if without end. All the kindness Ian had shown her, the promises he had made, the happiness he had given her.

He had not lied, not really. She was at fault, reading more into his goodness toward her and in wishing for what was out of her reach. Her friends, dear as they were to her, were wrong. God did not mean for her to have the kind of love and family that had always eluded her. God was surely watching over her, but what He wanted for her was a mystery, one she did not understand.

I'm trusting You, Lord. There has to be some good to come from this.

She unlatched the door and eased the buckets into the lean-to, to be dealt with during her morning chores. The storm blasted her with snow so that she was dusted white and her teeth chattered by the time she shut the door.

"Is that you, girl?" Da's shout was rusty with sleep and slurred from his drinking.

"Yes, sir." She crept into the fall of lamplight, stomach knotting over what he might say.

"Put some more coal on the fire. I'm gettin' cold." He rose from his chair, like an old man, one far past his prime. Sad it was he had wasted whatever had once been good in him, but that had been his choice. "I don't want you goin' to school in the morning, you hear? There's no sense to it anymore. You will be helping your ma with the housework from now on."

An angry gust slammed against the north wall of the room, shaking the window glass in its panes. Smoke puffed down the pipe and rattled the door. Without a word she knelt before the old potbelly, filled the scoop from the hod and opened the door handle with the hem of her apron. Heat and smoke made her eyes burn as she poured coal into the glowing embers.

Da said nothing more as he cracked open the seal on a new bottle. "What are you lookin' at?" he snarled.

"Good night." She closed the door, and it was like her fate sealing. When she stood, she felt light-headed and her knees were unsteady as she crossed the room. The cold deepened and the storm worsened. The howling wind filled the kitchen like a wild animal on the loose.

Ian was surely tucked in the barn by now. But that was little comfort as she climbed the ladder. Never before had she been so torn between what was right and what she wanted. She'd never known there were so many shades of gray between right and wrong. For if she ran with the few dollars that would be left in her savings after paying for Ian's coat, she would be without a job or anywhere to go. If she did not marry him, Ian would lose all he had and his grandmother's dreams—she did not fool herself by thinking her father would fairly return an old woman's money.

But how could she agree to marry a man who did not love her? A man who would marry her only because she came with a farm he wanted? Ian would always be kind to her, because that was the brand of man he was, but she could not be happy living her mother's life. At what cost did she refuse? Would the cost be greater if she accepted?

Worse, she did not want to spend twenty years of her life secretly in love with a man whose kindness to her was not affection, whose thoughtfulness was not devotion, whose heart would not be hers. It would be no happy ending, just a compromise, a business to gain land. Worse, she could not blame Ian, for he had the best excuse.

He had done it out of love.

Chapter Seventeen

At the toll of the schoolhouse bell, Fiona lifted her skirts higher and broke into a run. Snow blinded her, the icy flakes needled her face and the chilly air burned like fire in her chest. A hitch bit into her side, but she kept going. While she had been hurrying as fast as she could, it hadn't been quick enough. School had let out, and that meant in a few minutes' time, if she didn't reach the streets of town first, she would meet schoolchildren on their way home. She shut out images of kids asking her where she had been this morning and why she'd missed class. The notion of meeting Earlee on the road and having to explain, of seeing pity on her friend's face, made her miss a step.

She pushed harder until the houses on the

edge of town appeared through the shroud of white. She didn't slow to a walk until her shoes hit the boardwalk and she was just another person hurrying about her errands. Safe in the crowds of Christmas shoppers, she wove her way to the bank, where wreaths hung festively from the impressive wood awning, and garlands added holiday cheer to the front windows. Cheer that was at odds with her.

"Fiona? Is that you?" A familiar voice broke above the rush and bustle of the busy street.

Earlee. Fiona stopped in her tracks, dread filling her. What was she going to say to her friend? Some things were too painful to speak of.

"I was so worried about you." Earlee tapped closer, all friendly concern. "Are you all right?"

"I am fine." *Fine* was a relative term, but it was all she could manage.

"What are you doing here in town, and not at school?" Earlee looked her over carefully and appeared relieved, perhaps that there were no fresh bruises. "Is everything okay at home?"

"Fine." There was that word again. It was

not fine, but it was all she seemed able to say. "What are you doing in town?"

"Bea is ailing." Good-natured, Earlee rolled her eyes. "I have to stop and pick up some medicine. You haven't answered my question."

"I'm running errands for Ma."

"Is she feeling poorly?"

"No." Somehow she had to put a smile on her face and keep pretending she wasn't hurting. Maybe then she could convince herself. After all, falling in love with Ian wasn't the first foolish mistake she'd made, and life went on. Right?

"You *are* having trouble at home again." Earlee wrapped her in a brief hug, all sympathy, all caring. That was Earlee. A good friend through and through. "Is there something I can do?"

"No, I—" Her smile was faltering, no matter how she fought. "There's nothing. Really."

"I have today's homework assignments. Tomorrow we might have a quiz."

"I don't need them," she interrupted, too abruptly, too harshly, hating that she made her friend stare at her in surprise. "I'm sorry, I just—"

"It's okay. Tell me what is hurting you so."

I thought Ian was in love with me. I thought he was different from the men I know. I believed what he told me. I fell in love with him, and he only wanted the farm. Just like what happened to my ma. I'm afraid I will have the same life and as much unhappiness. She wanted to say all of that, but too many people were hurrying by with their Christmas shopping packages and seasonal cheer. Singing erupted down the street—the church caroling group. How could she speak of her private heartbreak where anyone could overhear?

"My parents think I don't need to finish school. That I need to stay home and learn how to be a wife." She sounded wooden to her ears, but at least her emotions did not show.

"Oh, Fee. I'm sorry." Earlee understood. "Being able to graduate meant so much to you."

"Yes, but there are other things to consider." Duty. What was right. What was merely being selfish. Once, she had been sure about those things. But her heart was involved now; she could not say Ian's dreams were more important than hers. She could not say her dreams were expendable, either.

"Is it Ian?"

"It's complicated." Fiona caught sight of

a familiar face across the street. The sheriff must be keeping an eye on her for Da. Dismayed, she turned her back to him. "I'm sorry, I have to go. Ma will be waiting for me."

"I have to make haste, too. Where are you heading to next? I'll meet you there, and we can hurry home together. We don't have to talk if you don't want to."

"Thanks. I really need a friend right now." She swallowed against the tightness in her throat. Those pesky emotions were troubling her again.

"I will always be here for you, Fee. You can count on me, right?"

"I know." What would she do without her friends? She let Earlee hug her one more time. With the closing verse of "O Come All Ye Faithful" accompanying them, Earlee broke off toward the dry-goods store. With one last wave goodbye, Fiona disappeared into the bank.

His thigh bone felt as if it had been hit by dynamite. He slid from Flannigan's broad back in the shadow of the barn, doing his level best to ignore the burning pain. Teeth gritted, he hauled the door open and led the horse inside. The day had been long, the work hard, but he was thankful for it. He had not expected to find a job so easily.

"I'm sorry it was a hard walk home, boy." He patted Flannigan's neck. The gelding lipped his hand, tired too. "I'll give you a good rubdown and treat you to some of Duchess's oats. You like warm mash?"

Horse ears flicked forward, pricked and eager. Answer enough.

"That's a good boy." He swiped off the snow gathered on the animal's mane and flanks. "I will make your bed up nice and thick for a good night's sleep. We must get up and do the same thing tomorrow."

A meow cried out from the beam overhead. Riley poked his nose over his gate. Duchess nickered low in her throat from some comfortable place inside her stall. The cow, chewing her cud, placidly leaned against her gate to see what all was going on. A welcoming committee of sorts and fine it was, but short one important person.

"It's late, sorry to bother you all." He half expected to see Fiona lean down from the haymow with bits of grass in her hair, or to scowl at him for disturbing her in her secluded spot in that far stall. Aye, he knew it was late, she would most likely be abed, but that didn't stop his hope. He wanted to speak with her.

You should bring her here. Her advice about Nana had preoccupied him the day through. *From what you have told me, she could never be disappointed in you. She loves you, and she is family. That is what matters.*

Aye, family was what mattered to him. He had always remained fiercely loyal to the grandparents who had raised him when his own father had refused. Now was his time to take care of them, to repay them for all the wise lessons in horses and life he had learned at his grandfather's side and for the gentler teachings of his strong, ever kind nana. He unbuckled Flannigan's halter, removing the bit with care.

"And how am I to do that?" He voiced his concern to the horse, who swiveled his ears as if to listen intently. "If I do not marry Fiona, then I have failed, good and truly. I cannot bring my mares out here if I have no land for them. I cannot make my grandmother happy in her last days without knowing their legacy lives on. If I make the lass marry me, then I have my chance to rebuild. I know I can do it. I am not afraid of the work it will take."

Flannigan must have sensed his turmoil, because the big horse leaned into him, pressing his face against Ian's chest. An intimate, comforting gesture. Touched by the fellow's concern, he leaned his cheek against the horse's forehead, savoring the coarse scratchiness of the animal's forelock.

Perhaps it was the long hard day of physical work or that he was infinitely tired of fighting for someone else's dreams, but his defenses were down, his soul weary. He had failed Fiona, too. He wanted to blame his grandmother for interfering again, but what good could come of that? Every mistake he had made along the way smarted like deep, unhealed wounds. He had pushed himself to the limit, working to make things right and following where he thought the Lord was guiding him, but he was at a dead end. There would be no good solution, whatever he chose to do. He would lose his grandmother's faith in him, or he would ruin Fiona's chance for happiness.

How did he choose?

The past was good and truly gone. Maybe that was what God has been trying to tell him, closing all doors but this one and bringing him here to Fiona's sad life, the girl he had been destined to marry in his grandparents' dreams. Maybe, if the good Lord had led him here, then it was not the past he needed to build on, but a different future.

"I feel as if I am letting down those I have loved the most." He released Flannigan, but the horse didn't move away. With his liquid brown eyes and intent stare, he seemed to care a great deal about the outcome, too. "Maybe the best way to repay my grandparents' legacy of love is to do what I think is right."

Flannigan stomped his front hoof as if in agreement, as if to say it was truly time to let go, that no one should hold on to the past so tightly that he destroyed what is good in life and in his future. Sometimes a man had to follow the hardest path, no matter its cost.

"What a good friend you are, boy." He stroked the animal's feather-soft nose, warm with affection for the old boy. "You have not had an easy time. I know O'Rourke is a hard master to you, and you have not deserved it. A truer heart I have never met. You've the spirit of a champion, my friend."

In appreciation, the draft horse lipped Ian's hat brim, earning a chuckle. "Let's get you rubbed down, so I can fetch the mash I promised. How does that sound?"

Flannigan nodded enthusiastically and took off for his stall. His tail flicked, waiting while Ian hurried to open the gate. The cat pranced along the rafters overhead, and Riley leaned out for attention and perhaps to ask for mash, too.

This would be a good life, he decided, glancing around at the small barn, the handful of livestock and the memories of Fiona lingering here. Aye, the lass had changed him. His love for her drove him now as he clenched his jaw against the ever-present pain in his leg and kept his voice gentle as he rubbed down Flannigan until he was dry and warm. She was the reason he had the strength to make the hardest decision, the one best for them both.

The evenings were the worst, Fiona decided as she guided her needle through the thick fabric with a click of her thimble. Her chores were done, and with the weather taking an unusually brutal turn, her fingers went numb every time she tried sewing in the barn. She missed her animal friends and the sanctuary she once had found there, but it was gone now and the place a reminder of the cost she was to pay. She had not run; she had paid Miss Sims what she owed her, although she was sure if she explained the situation, the fair lady would have gladly taken back the fabric. No, sewing this coat was the right thing. Ian had sacrificed Duchess's foal for her, a foal Ian surely loved and wanted.

He should have his dreams. She pressed the seam flat with her fingers, careful of the pins holding the fabric, and memories of him filled her mind. How thrilling it had felt to gallop with him through the snow in the sled, and the joy that filled her when he had given her Flannigan's reins. Every smile, every chuckle, and the afternoon he had given her at the church. Even his promises that for a moment she feared were false—that he had come back to help her, that he cared about her dreams, all of it she knew he had meant.

The trouble was, some things mattered to him more. That was simply the way life was. She had fallen in love with him, and that love made her wish for what could never be. She was not going to marry Ian, but neither was she going to run from her problems.

The candle on her bureau chose that moment to flicker. The wind gusted again, blow-ing through the cracks in the wall, nearly dousing it. The flame writhed as if in pain, and she squinted, trying to see enough for her next stitch. Iciness crept through the floor and roof above, and the next gust extinguished the candle.

The night closed in on her, and the hopelessness that always chased her caught up. Without her dreams of running away to escape into, without her brother who had always lent a kind word of understanding, with only the present and this life stretching ahead of her forever, she had nothing to console her. She put down her work, pressed her face in her hands and breathed deep, fighting not to give in to it.

A rush of wind howled through the house, rattling the glass chimney of the lamp in the kitchen and ghosting up the ladder. She shivered, realizing she wasn't alone. An uneven gait padded on squeaky floorboards. The oven door creaked open.

Ian, home for the night. How was he? She had not seen him for days. She crept off the foot of the bed and along the floor, knowing which boards to avoid so she could move in silence. She stretched out on her stomach, easing up to peer over the edge of the doorway. The kitchen stretched out before her, black as a void except for the glow of orange lapping from the open oven door and onto the man seated before it.

He had drawn one of the chairs over to the heat, and, still coated in snow and ice, held his hands out to the warmth, rubbing to thaw them. The building fire tossed ever brighter light over the man, who remained in silhouette as he hunched toward the warmth. Cold radiated from him, but so did his strength and his goodness. He made no sound of discomfort, although he had to be frozen clean through.

More affection dawned within her, as wonderful and as blessed as Christmas morning. She eased into the safe shadows, hidden from his sight. Love for him bloomed fully, like grace falling into her life. It was a love never meant to be returned, she feared, but one that would always live inside her heart.

Chapter Eighteen

"Fiona! You made it." Lila greeted her in a warm hug before tugging her into the lovely parlor. "Look, everyone. She's here."

"We didn't think you were going to come." Scarlet bolted up from a chair and hugged her, too. "You look frozen clean through."

"Come sit in my seat." Earlee hopped off the edge of the couch. "It's closest to the fireplace."

"Things weren't going to be the same without you, Fee." Kate stood to hug her, as well.

"I had just made up my mind to drive out to fetch you." Meredith took her by the hands and led her to the seat Earlee had vacated. "We are all so glad you could come."

"I almost didn't." Fiona clutched her satchel and her book bag, both stiff with frost from the walk to town. Actually, it had been a run-walk, hurrying as fast as she could and hoping no one came riding after her. "My parents forbade me, but I couldn't stay away. I have missed you all so much."

"We have missed you, too," Scarlet and Kate chorused, and Earlee took her hand in silent agreement.

"I have had to sit at our desk all by myself. During class I start scribbling a note to you on my slate, and realize you aren't there." Lila poured a cup of tea from the service on the coffee table. "School isn't the same without you, Fee."

Her throat burned, and she felt out of place, the outsider in this group where she had always belonged. She was no longer a schoolgirl like they were. Everything within her yearned to go back. If only it were possible.

"I know how you feel." Meredith took the bags from her and set them on the floor, near to the hearth, so they would thaw out. "Every day I have spent away from you all is a form of misery. Mama thinks she is doing right by sending me away to school, but I'm happiest when I am with my best friends."

"Remember how we all met?" Lila squeezed

in to hand over the steaming china cup of sweet tea.

"In first-grade Sunday school." Earlee settled into a chair. "Remember? My ma had just left me there. I was the first little girl to arrive, and I was afraid to stay with Mrs. Hadly. Then Scarlet came marching up with her ma. You took one look at me and said—"

"—you are my friend," Scarlet finished, laughing. She settled on the cushion beside Fiona with a flourish. "I have always been forthright. It appalls Ma to this day. Anyway, the next kid to come along was Narcissa Bell. I didn't like the way she wrinkled her nose at me and said my dress was, what did she say?"

"'Common calico,'" Lila supplied as she lifted the china teapot and began refilling everyone's cups. "As I love calico and was wearing the new rosebud-sprigged dress my mother had lovingly made for me, I took great offense."

"And I told Narcissa she was *not* my friend."

"You were an excellent judge of character, even at six years of age." Meredith stole a sugar cube from the service and handed the bowl to Fiona. "I can see you all arriving in your cute little dresses and Scarlet telling each one of you that you were her friend."

"It was the first time I was with children my own age." Fiona remembered how terrified she had been when Ma had left her at the bottom of the basement steps. "I couldn't make my feet move. I felt everyone looking at me. So when Scarlet strode forward and took my hand, I thought she was wonderful, that you were all so amazing for wanting me."

"Same thing with me," Earlee confessed. "Who would have thought that first Sunday-school class what, twelve years ago, would be the start of lifelong friendships?"

"One of God's great blessings," Kate agreed, and swiped a tear from the corner of her eye.

"Which is why I am not going back to Boston." Meredith's confession raised shocked comments from them all. "I have been utterly miserable there, and I haven't known what to do about it or how to make Mama understand. But listening to you all has made me realize something. I have never been happier since the day I walked into Sunday school almost five years ago and you all invited me to sit with you."

"Narcissa Bell and her group wanted you,

too." Fiona sipped the steaming tea, but that wasn't what warmed her. Her friends and their memories together did. "Remember? You were a vision in that gown of yours. I've never seen anything prettier."

"Not even Narcissa had anything so nice," Earlee added. "What I remember was how you held your sisters' hands, like you were all close. And how Mrs. Hadly split you up by age. I could tell you and your sisters didn't like it, and that's how I knew you would fit in just fine with us, although we weren't so fancy."

"That's what I thought, too," Scarlet added.

"It's going to be fun to have you back in school," Kate said thoughtfully as she picked up her sewing. "But it comes at the same time we are losing Fiona."

"Maybe you can still come to our sewing circle?" Lila asked as she threaded her needle.

"I wish I could." She slid her cup and saucer onto the edge of the table and reached for her bag. She unfolded her work and settled it on her lap.

"That's beautiful." Earlee leaned forward to examine the fabric. "Is that something you're working on for Miss Sims?"

"No, it's a Christmas present. For Ian."

She smoothed the lapel lovingly. The seam was sitting well, and she couldn't help being pleased with her work. "He will be bringing out his herd of mares soon, and I want him to have a warm riding coat. Something suited to the stature I'm sure his ranch will soon be."

"*His* ranch?" Scarlet's embroidery needle stilled. "Does this mean you will be marrying him for real?"

"And soon?" Meredith looked up from pinning a quilt block seam.

"No. Ian does not love me, so he shouldn't be forced to marry me. And you all know how I feel about marriage. I'm not going to be tethered down." She didn't believe in love, right? She was the girl who had never started sewing treasures for a hope chest. The last thing she would ever trust in was a man's love for her.

And if a tiny voice deep within her wanted to argue, she silenced it entirely.

"But you are in love with him." Earlee, ever the romantic, put down her crocheting.

"I don't intend to let any man own or dominate me, not even Ian." She ran her fingertips over the coat, remembering how Miss Sims had helped her with the pattern and had even cut it for her. How she had spent her evenings pinning the pieces, basting them and stitching each seam with care. She had fitted the collar and sleeves, imagining him astride one of his beautiful mares or training a young colt in the corral.

In truth, the reason she loved Ian was simple: he was not the kind of man to dominate a woman. But this was a celebration, and not a place for her disappointments, so she kept silent about them. "When are we going to exchange gifts? I am so excited for you all to see what I made for you."

"Oh, me, too!" Scarlet twisted around to tug a bag off the floor. "As is our tradition, I made something for each of our hope chests. Even Fiona's, although she refuses to have a real hope chest."

"That's okay, Fee. We will keep hoping for you when you are out of faith." Earlee put five equal-size gifts wrapped in newsprint in the center of the table.

"We will keep praying for you when you stop praying for yourself." Lila rescued five identical gifts wrapped in lovely wrapping paper and put them beside Earlee's.

"We want you to be happy," Kate added, gathering her gifts from her sewing basket.

"Even if you can't keep coming to our sewing circle, we will keep a place open for you. Just like we did for Meredith." Scarlet added five more gaily wrapped presents to the growing pile.

"We will be here for you, Fee." Meredith crossed the room to fetch her bag full of gifts. "Always and forever."

Fiona looked from one dear face to the other—her family, in all the ways that mattered. There were those pesky feelings again, making her far too vulnerable and trying to blur her vision. Touched by the amazing wealth of friendship, she saw for the first time the incredible richness of her life.

Ian knew the moment the sun set. The storm changed, the air turned reverent and the snowflakes floated through the air solemnly. Flannigan, warm in his stall, snorted, as if he could scent night's approach. Duchess cast an anxious gaze down the aisle, for this place was not home to her.

"We won't be here for much longer, so rest easy," he told his mare and gave the pitchfork a final turn. He had rented a two-room house north of town, closer to his job. A place Nana might like, and the owner did not mind if he improved on the fencing. A better place for his future than this broken-down farm of neglect and sadness. The cow patiently chewed at the fresh hay in her feeder. He patted her flank with his gloved hand, to slide behind her and out of the stall. "I'll be back to milk you, sweet girl."

The cow blinked her liquid-brown eyes in agreement, content with her dinner.

The cat, however, was not so pleased. He yowled underfoot.

"I've not forgotten you, you mop." Affectionate, he knelt to give the feline a fine scrub around the ears. The rusty, ardent purr was reward enough. "I'll get to the milking next."

He felt Fiona's presence before he heard her—the tug as if a door opened within him, the sweetness of first love, the brightness of hope stirring. The day was no longer ordinary. At the pad of her footsteps, he looked up to see her approaching the open barn door. Snowflakes danced around her as if glad to be with her. The twilight was perfect because she walked through it.

Flannigan nickered, perhaps in love with her, too. Not ashamed to show it, the gelding leaned hard until the wood gate dug into his flesh and stretched his long neck as far as he could go, craning to get a view of her. Riley, with a mouthful of hay, followed suit, and the cow gave a hopeful moo. Even Duchess in her corner stall offered a welcoming nicker and the cat raced the length of the barn as if eager for the privilege of curling around her ankles.

"Good evening to you, handsome boy. I'm glad to see you, too." She knelt, her hood shading her face, elegant in her thick woolen wraps.

Ian, eager to see the first glimpse of her face, knew he was standing in the aisle like one of the posts, still and staring, but did he care? No, not one bit. He would cherish all he could of this time left with her.

"McPherson. What are you doing here?" She straightened and although he could not see her face, he felt the sting of her glare. "I thought you would be at work."

"What? You are afraid I am like your father, unable to hold a job?" Tender, he saw what she thought of him; he could not help teasing her. "No. The mill closed at noon. It is Christmas Eve, after all."

"I didn't know you would be here." Her arms were full, and a bag hung from her shoulder, thick and heavy. "I just came in from town."

"Were you with your friends, like last week? At Lila's, is that her name?"

"Yes." She pulled back her hood, icy crystals tumbling from the fabric to rain down at her feet. Flecked with snow, she looked like a storybook princess, too beautiful to be real and too good to want to be with a man like him.

That didn't stop him from hoping.

"We had our own Christmas celebration. I got a lot of beautiful things for the hope chest I don't have." The lantern light found her, bathing her with its luminous glow. She tripped forward to lay her bundle and bag on the grain-barrel lid. "My tatted doilies and matching snowflake ornaments were very well received. Why don't I finish the chores? You have had a hard week, Ian."

"One I am grateful for. I have a good-paying job." He winced at the signs of exhaustion on her face—the shadows smudging the porcelain skin beneath her eyes, and the strain etched into her forehead. He shoved his hand in his pocket to resist the urge to try to smooth them away. All he wanted was to draw her into his arms and shelter her, hold her until she understood everything was going to be all right. "I will finish the barn work, lass. But first, there's something I want to give you."

"You mean, like a gift?"

"It *is* Christmas Eve." A dapper man would know what to say to win her heart. A smart man would know the right way to let her go. But as he was neither dapper nor smart, he pulled the train ticket from his coat pocket. "This is for you. Merry Christmas."

"I don't understand." She took the first-class permit, staring at it as if she didn't know how to read. "You want me to go and fetch your grandmother?"

"No, pretty girl." He cradled her chin in his palm, unable to hold back the tidal force of his affection. "This is to take you anywhere you want. I am not going to make you marry me. You are free to go."

"But the farm. Your grandmother paid my da—"

"That she did." He prayed she would never know how hard this was for him, all that he had given up for her. "Your father and I have come to final terms this afternoon and there will be no marriage. You need never worry about being forced to live your mother's life. You and Flannigan are free."

"Flannigan?" Her lower lip trembled; he

rubbed the pad of his thumb along her plump bottom lip.

"He is yours. I paid your father for him."

"But your wages were to go for your mares." Instead of the joy he expected, her sorrow deepened, and the shadows swallowed her, as if she had lost the last bit of hope.

"What is wrong?" Her sadness splintered him into pieces. "You promised to take him with you. I heard you tell him so the day he tried to run away."

"But what about you, Ian?"

"My dreams have changed." If he had thought her beauty great before, it was nothing to her comeliness as the lantern light flared. He knew how that light felt, unable to let go, unable to keep her. "Some things in life are not to be, no matter how much you want them. If I can't have what I wish, then you will have your happiness."

He could not help it, he was a besotted man and he wanted her to feel—not just to know—how he cared for her. He leaned forward and brushed her mouth with his. Sweeter than Christmas candy, that kiss, and he savored it—savored her—before he moved away. The memory of it was the last he would have of her.

It took all his strength to withdraw his fingers from her chin, to step back and hitch up his dignity. No sense letting the girl know how foolish in love he was with her. "Go follow your dream, Fiona."

Chapter Nineteen

"What about your grandmother's money?" She could not think straight. The gentle bliss of Ian's kiss had muddled her mind, and she could not gather it enough to make sense of what he was saying. She only knew that her father would not let her go out of any sense of Christmas spirit. "I can't allow her to be swindled on my behalf. She was my grandmother's best friend, I know the value of that bond. I do not want to dishonor their friendship. She has paid for the property. Did my father sign over the deed to you?"

"No, he did not." The steely mask that Ian kept in place slid away, just a second's weakness, and she saw the truth and felt it settle in her soul. The bond between them remained, stronger than ever, and she caught his hand with hers, his so much larger and capable of accomplishing so much. She thought of the horses he had been destined to train, champions yet to be proven, and his gentle horseman's nature. He had sacrificed much for that future. She hated that it would be delayed again.

"There might be another farm? You have a good job. Is that what you are hoping for?"

"No. That road is no longer meant for me." His fingers twined through hers, locking them together, and that felt like destiny, too. "I sent a draft to Nana to reimburse her for the money. The original offer was for you, not the land. Do you remember?"

"But you wanted the land."

"No. I want you."

To have her dream, she finished for him. To take the ticket and leave town, she told her impossibly rising hopes. Not because he loved her. He did not mean he wanted her and he loved her and he felt an endless, abiding devotion, too. Her lips tingled, proof of his kiss—goodbye? Was that why he had kissed her? As a farewell gesture?

Of course, it had to be. She stared at the ticket in her hand. She was the one holding on to him. She was the one with lead feet, unable to move. Wasn't she the one who had fallen? And yet his grip tightened, his fingers clutching hers. As if he did not want to let go.

Hope lifted on wings within her. All the things he had done for her, all that he had said came back to her anew.

"Where did you get the money?"

"I sold my mares, all but Duchess." His throat worked, and his granite mask was back in place. Only the tic of tension in his set jaw revealed the cost of that decision.

"You sold your thoroughbreds? No. I don't believe it." She couldn't make her brain accept it. "You couldn't have. They mean everything to you."

"Not everything." Tender, those words, and layered with something more, something deeper. "I did it for you, Fiona."

"For me?" A terrible cracking rent through her, the last of her denial, the last of her old, useless beliefs she had been clinging to. That there were no noble men, that no man would love her, that she did not believe in love. Those notions shattered like glass, their shards landing on the dirt at her feet, useless and impossible to pick up. Falsehoods she could no longer believe in.

"Midweek I sent a telegram to my friend,

the one keeping what was left of my herd." No sorrow rang in the deep notes of his voice. Only peace. "Jack was happy to buy them."

What did she believe in? Ian. She believed in his noble heart, in his compassionate spirit and in the love polishing him in the lantern's coppery light.

"You have to get them back." She tore her hand from his, whirling away. "This isn't right, what you've done."

"What isn't right about it? It is the best thing for you."

"But what about you?" She had been prepared to care for her parents, find a job in town to help support them and do her share of the work forever, if it meant Ian could have his land. Was it too late to give him what he wanted most? What he deserved? "If you take Flannigan right now and hurry to town, you can make it before the depot closes. You can send a wire and get your mares back."

"Dear, sweet Fiona." He came to her, both comfort and might. No sorrow shadowed his gaze, for there was a greater emotion, one pure enough that nothing could mask it. "Do not be so upset for me. I am glad to do this. I have been able to pay the last of my grandparents' debts. My burden is lighter."

"But I could see them here, those beautiful horses like Duchess grazing in these perfect green fields, their coats of every color gleaming in the sunshine. And you—" Her breath hitched, betraying her sorrow for him. He might not be sad, but she was. "You were supposed to train them and prosper. I know you will be successful. I see you, Ian, all of you, your goodness and your gentleness. Horses love you. Look at Flannigan. He behaved terribly most of the time. He was afraid of men, all save my brother, and you came along and turned him into a kitten. Look at him. He adores you."

"The feeling is mutual."

For a moment it did not seem as if he were speaking of the horse. More hope rushed in, making her long for the impossible—a lifetime loving him.

"So you can go with good conscience now, lass. I will be well. My grandmother will be able to buy back her family jewelry. And you can have that little house somewhere with flowers all around it."

"I cannot go," she confessed. "I spent all but five dollars of my savings."

"On what?"

"Your Christmas gift." She broke away

from him, the silence of the barn echoing like a great stillness. The animals had quieted, watching intently. Mally, sitting on a stall rail, did not blink. Not even his tail moved as she opened her bag to withdraw the finished garment. "It's the warmest fabric I could find. A riding coat, for working with your horses."

"The horses I do not have?"

"Yes."

"Ah, lass, but you have touched me. You have captured me heart and soul. How am I to let you go now?"

"Do you not want me to go? But you sold your horses so I can leave you. This train ticket—"

"No, my love. I want you to be free to choose." He brushed her cheeks with his thumb, and her tears glimmered on his glove. "Remember I said that a marriage between us always has been your decision and no other's?"

"I do. I choose you, Ian McPherson. You have made me believe in true love and noble men."

"And happily-ever-afters," he finished. Not sadness, then, driving those tears, but the same poignant emotion driving him. He felt it when she laid her hand on his chest, her small hand over his heart. He loved her; the infinite gentleness he felt for her had no bounds, no ends, no reason.

Happiness roared through him, strong enough to drown out all his old losses, and he knew that the past was gone. There was a future to build, the only one that mattered, the one God had led him to. For surely it was God's presence gentle in the air above them, and in the proof of their love so strong. "I cannot give you a mansion full of fine things and servants."

"I would not want it if you could." In her perfect blue eyes, on her beloved face, her love shone for him. Unmistakable and the greatest gift he could imagine. The best Christmas gift on this holy night of love and saving grace. She smiled up at him, their hearts and souls as one. "A little house someday, with a happy family. All I want is for you to love me, Ian, and I will have the greatest of all riches."

"We will be very wealthy indeed." He drew her into the circle of his arms, where she was safe, where she would always be cherished and protected. "Marry me, Fiona. Be my treasured wife."

"It would be an honor."

Their kiss was perfection, as pure as the night. The winds stilled and the last flakes of snow tapered gently to the ground. Heavenly moonlight fell between the breaking clouds as if to bless the love of a worthy horseman and his gingham bride.

* * * * *

Dear Reader,

Welcome back to Angel Falls. This Montana town has become a beloved place to me, full of fond friends and new ones yet to meet. I hope you feel the same way. In this story, you will see familiar faces, like Cora and her nephews (from *A Blessed Season*) and new ones, like Fiona and her friends.

Gingham Bride is a story I have been wanting to tell for a long time. It is a tale of how love comes to a girl who has not known it before and the good man who can win her heart. I hope you are touched by Fiona's journey, Ian's sacrifice for her and their discovery of the true riches God has blessed them with. Meredith's story is next!

Thank you for choosing GINGHAM BRIDE.

Wishing you the best of blessings.

Merry Christmas,

Jillian Hart

QUESTIONS FOR DISCUSSION

1. Describe Ian's reaction the first time her sees Fiona. Do you think this is love at first sight? What does he see in her that no one else does?

2. How would you describe Fiona's opinion of most men? How would you describe her first impressions of Ian? What does she see that is different about him?

3. Why does Ian decide to stay with Fiona? Why do you think he has come to this decision? What sacrifices has he made for her? What does this say about his character?

4. How do you think the past has influenced Ian? Why can't he let go of the past?

5. How do you think Fiona's childhood has influenced her? Why does she cling so hard to the idea of a future alone? What does this say about her character?

6. What is the story's predominant imagery? How does it contribute to the meaning of the story?

7. Fiona is not sure how God works in her life. Ian tries to follow where the Lord is leading him but is unsure how it can end well. How do these issues of faith develop for each character? How are they resolved?

8. When we first meet Fiona, she is determined not to trust in love and believes there are no noble men. How does Ian change that? How does he touch her heart?

9. How is God's leading evident in the story?

10. What do you think Fiona and Ian have each learned about the power of hope?

11. What values of Christmas do you find in this story? What do those values mean to you?

12. What do you think of Ian's Christmas gift to Fiona, and of hers to him? What does this say to you about the kind of love they share? What do you think they have learned about love?

REQUEST YOUR FREE BOOKS!

2 FREE INSPIRATIONAL NOVELS
PLUS 2
FREE
MYSTERY GIFTS

Love Inspired®

REQUEST YOUR FREE BOOKS!
2 FREE RIVETING INSPIRATIONAL NOVELS
PLUS 2 FREE MYSTERY GIFTS

Love Inspired®
SUSPENSE
RIVETING·INSPIRATIONAL·ROMANCE

YES! Please send me 2 FREE Love Inspired® Suspense novels and my 2 FREE mystery gifts (gifts are worth about $10). After receiving them, if I don't wish to receive any more books, I can return the shipping statement marked "cancel." If I don't cancel, I will receive 4 brand-new novels every month and be billed just $4.99 per book in the U.S. or $5.49 per book in Canada. That's a savings of at least 17% off the cover price. It's quite a bargain! Shipping and handling is just 50¢ per book in the U.S. and 75¢ per book in Canada.* I understand that accepting the 2 free books and gifts places me under no obligation to buy anything. I can always return a shipment and cancel at any time. Even if I never buy another book, the two free books and gifts are mine to keep forever.

123/323 IDN GH5Z

Name _____ (PLEASE PRINT)

Address _____ Apt. #

City _____ State/Prov. _____ Zip/Postal Code

Signature (if under 18, a parent or guardian must sign)

Mail to the **Reader Service**:
IN U.S.A.: P.O. Box 1867, Buffalo, NY 14240-1867
IN CANADA: P.O. Box 609, Fort Erie, Ontario L2A 5X3

**Are you a current subscriber to Love Inspired® Suspense books
and want to receive the larger-print edition?
Call 1-800-873-8635 or visit www.ReaderService.com.**

* Terms and prices subject to change without notice. Prices do not include applicable taxes. Sales tax applicable in N.Y. Canadian residents will be charged applicable taxes. Offer not valid in Quebec. This offer is limited to one order per household. Not valid for current subscribers to Love Inspired Suspense books. All orders subject to credit approval. Credit or debit balances in a customer's account(s) may be offset by any other outstanding balance owed by or to the customer. Please allow 4 to 6 weeks for delivery. Offer available while quantities last.

Your Privacy—The Reader Service is committed to protecting your privacy. Our Privacy Policy is available online at www.ReaderService.com or upon request from the Reader Service.
We make a portion of our mailing list available to reputable third parties that offer products we believe may interest you. If you prefer that we not exchange your name with third parties, or if you wish to clarify or modify your communication preferences, please visit us at www.ReaderService.com/consumerchoice or write to us at Reader Service Preference Service, P.O. Box 9062, Buffalo, NY 14240-9062. Include your complete name and address.

LIS15

REQUEST YOUR FREE BOOKS!

2 FREE INSPIRATIONAL NOVELS
PLUS 2 FREE MYSTERY GIFTS

Love Inspired® H I S T O R I C A L

YES! Please send me 2 FREE Love Inspired® Historical novels and my 2 FREE mystery gifts (gifts are worth about $10). After receiving them, if I don't wish to receive any more books, I can return the shipping statement marked "cancel." If I don't cancel, I will receive 4 brand-new novels every month and be billed just $4.99 per book in the U.S. or $5.49 per book in Canada. That's a saving of at least 17% off the cover price. It's quite a bargain! Shipping and handling is just 50¢ per book in the U.S. and 75¢ per book in Canada.* I understand that accepting the 2 free books and gifts places me under no obligation to buy anything. I can always return a shipment and cancel at any time. Even if I never buy another book, the two free books and gifts are mine to keep forever.

102/302 IDN GH6Z

Name	(PLEASE PRINT)	
Address		Apt. #
City	State/Prov.	Zip/Postal Code

Signature (if under 18, a parent or guardian must sign)

Mail to the **Reader Service:**
IN U.S.A.: P.O. Box 1867, Buffalo, NY 14240-1867
IN CANADA: P.O. Box 609, Fort Erie, Ontario L2A 5X3

Want to try two free books from another series?
Call 1-800-873-8635 or visit www.ReaderService.com.

* Terms and prices subject to change without notice. Prices do not include applicable taxes. Sales tax applicable in N.Y. Canadian residents will be charged applicable taxes. Offer not valid in Quebec. This offer is limited to one order per household. Not valid for current subscribers to Love Inspired Historical books. All orders subject to credit approval. Credit or debit balances in a customer's account(s) may be offset by any other outstanding balance owed by or to the customer. Please allow 4 to 6 weeks for delivery. Offer available while quantities last.

Your Privacy—The Reader Service is committed to protecting your privacy. Our Privacy Policy is available online at www.ReaderService.com or upon request from the Reader Service.

We make a portion of our mailing list available to reputable third parties that offer products we believe may interest you. If you prefer that we not exchange your name with third parties, or if you wish to clarify or modify your communication preferences, please visit us at www.ReaderService.com/consumerchoice or write to us at Reader Service Preference Service, P.O. Box 9062, Buffalo, NY 14240-9062. Include your complete name and address.

LIHI5

READERSERVICE.COM

Manage your account online!

- Review your order history
- Manage your payments
- Update your address

> ### We've designed the Reader Service website just for you.

Enjoy all the features!

- Discover new series available to you, and read excerpts from any series.
- Respond to mailings and special monthly offers.
- Connect with favorite authors at the blog.
- Browse the Bonus Bucks catalog and online-only exculsives.
- Share your feedback.

Visit us at:

ReaderService.com